Erin has spent the last 25 years in middle school. She earned a master's degree in Education and is twice National Board certified. She is a cross categorical teacher specializing in reading, writing, and social thinking, and is the mother of two teenage daughters. Writing and storytelling has been a lifelong project. This is her debut novel. *Between the Lines* was created to make social thinking part of reading and our everyday lives. Erin lives in Wisconsin and loves to travel with her husband and kids.

To Leah and Addie, with love.
Be smart, be kind

Erin Krase-Minchk

# BETWEEN THE LINES

AUSTIN MACAULEY PUBLISHERS™

LONDON * CAMBRIDGE * NEW YORK * SHARJAH

**Ordering Information**
Quantity sales: Special discounts are available on quantity purchases by corporations, associations, and others. For details, contact the publisher at the address below.

**Publisher's Cataloging-in-Publication data**

Krase-Minchk, Erin
Between the Lines

ISBN 9798886932676 (Paperback)
ISBN 9798886932683 (ePub e-book)

Library of Congress Control Number: 2023908505

www.austinmacauley.com/us

First Published 2023
Austin Macauley Publishers LLC
40 Wall Street,33rd Floor, Suite 3302
New York, NY 10005
USA

mail-usa@austinmacauley.com
+1 (646) 5125767

I would first like to thank my husband, Chris, for believing in me when I said, "I wrote a book!" You keep life full of adventures and provide the best tech support, which has been a great help during the writing process. I am grateful to have you by my side along this journey!

Thank you to my parents who, without hesitation, were my very first beta readers. Thank you for instilling in me a passion for learning, for teaching with kindness and grace, and a belief to follow my dreams.

Thank you to my daughters, Leah and Addie, who listened as I talked through ideas. You shared your feedback and views as I wrote. You helped me see the world through new eyes, and love being your mom!

Thank you, Joy Vangen, for being my first copy editor. Your outstanding editing skills helped clarify my words and the story in my heart.

Thank you to my beta readers who were willing to share their time and feedback. I am forever grateful! Thank you, Kim Amann, Tina Josephson, Erin Norris, Olivia Spader, Gracelyn Staude, and Jenny Steiner.

Lastly, I would like to thank Austin Macauley for helping me reach my dream of becoming a published author. Everyone from the editors and artists to the production managers and marketing staff have helped my vision come to life. Thank you!

# Table of Content

# Preface

We all have ideas in our heads and a lot to say to those around us. Anytime you are with another person, your ideas are mixed with theirs. Do they fit together like puzzle pieces? Or are the ideas so different that they repel each other like the matching ends of magnets? Or do the ideas start a disagreement? Your words, your actions, and your body language tell your ideas.

On the **flip side**, the person or people you are talking with also have ideas to share that are equally important. Understanding how to navigate and listen for tone, hidden meaning, and body language is big thinking work; especially when you want to get your own ideas out and be understood.

Written stories are one of the many ways to express ideas. Just like you, characters communicate with one another, and at times, are involved in conflicts. As readers, part of your job is to pay attention to how characters think, feel, and act. Thankfully, this book has built-in clues to help you navigate, or get through, the story. The clues will help you **dig deeper** into what is really happening in the characters 'lives. Anytime an idea is in bold (darker print), look between the lines at the end of each chapter. You will find information to help you figure out the social thinking that is part of the story. This is especially important since these ideas may not be specifically found in the words typed on the page.

As you read, take your time, think about the characters and their experiences, and dive into the bold statements because between the lines is where the characters' truths shine through. (Hint: The same is true for people you meet every day).

*If you are ready to push your thinking further, each chapter's title is a figure of speech that includes the word 'line' or is related to line(s). This means that the words in the chapter titles have a separate message beyond the words as they are printed. After you read each chapter, take time to think about what happened (plot), and connect the title to the plot, characters 'actions, and/or characters 'emotions.

Happy reading!


## Figurative Language

**Flip Side**: The reverse or opposite point of view.

**Dig Deeper**: To look at something carefully and find the big idea/message the words are really telling -you.

# Chapter 1
## Online

22% left.

I've been on my phone so much today. Almost all the battery life I have is gone. And my life? Also at 22% right now. Or at least that's how it feels. How did I get to this moment? Everything was planned so perfectly. I made sure everything was done on time. I made sure my group knew where to meet. I followed the directions. I listened to my group members. But I missed one thing. One really big, super important, **flashing-in-my-face clue.** And now, while all my friends enjoy our 8th grade celebration dance, I'm stuck here.

In my bed.

All night.

Wishing I were there inside every photo 'liked' on Instagram.

My dress, back in the bag, hanging on the closet door.

My shoes sticking out of the box. Still looking brand new.

But the blister on the back of my right heel is proof I wore them.

Mom's "Have some cocoa – you'll feel better cocoa" next to my bed.

Missing everything.

AND…

I think my little brother took my phone charger – AGAIN. The battery is draining with each swipe of post after post.

I wish I was there.

Social Thinking: We don't know why, but Lucy is missing out on something that means a lot to her. Watch for moments in the story to help you understand why she is so upset.


## Figurative Language

**Flashing-in-my-face clue** – sometimes, there are clues around us, but we just don't see them. They are not really flashing lights, but we compare them to this because it is likely everyone else has caught on to what is really going on. For example, I could say I didn't grab my umbrella despite the flashing-in-my-face clue of dark clouds overhead. The clouds are noticeable and easy to spot if one just looks up.

# Chapter 2
# Color Outside the Lines

"Don't look now, but I think Hayden just looked over at me," I say to Callie as she looks over, even though I told her not to. She always does this, no matter where we are. The after-school meeting to plan for the 8th grade promotion ceremony is no exception.

*Callie – stop!*

Callie doesn't listen to directions very well even though she should. I've been her best friend in the whole world since 1st grade. But she can be clueless when it comes to boys. She just stares at Hayden for way too long. I'm sure Hayden knows we are talking about him.

I lean into Callie and use my maddest whisper voice while still trying to be quiet. "Callie, can you make it any more obvious? He's looking right this way."

*Now what do I do? Should I wave, hide, smile…?*

Thankfully, Mr. Horvik pulls all eyes his way as he starts the meeting for our 8th grade promotion ceremony. I welcome this interruption that may save my sweaty armpits from causing an even bigger disaster in front of Hayden.

"Thank you all for coming this afternoon. The 8th grade promotion ceremony has always been an important milestone on your journey to high school graduation. As you know, this year, we are looking for students to present what it means to become a young adult in this age of technology, information overload, and innovation. All are welcome to participate, regardless of how much public speaking experience you have. I am grateful for your time and talents, but we also must work quickly."

*Wow! Teachers talk a lot, even after school.*

There are three eye rolls from students in the crowd when speaking experience is mentioned. The biggest offender is Elizabeth Saverin.

A **triple threat**, but also the prettiest girl in the 8th grade class. Rumor has it she was dating an actual Broadway star from the show Hamilton. But since it isn't likely a 14-year-old from the Milwaukee suburbs would be dating a Broadway star in New York, I'm guessing Elizabeth started the rumor just to up her own chances of getting more time to speak at the ceremony. And every community performance she is in. And, well, more attention, as always.

"Students, I have already taken the sign up list with your names, and I have assigned groups for you to work with. Your task will be to select a famous quote from my hat, develop a plan, and record a one-to-two-minute video presentation that can be added to our school video presentation. This will be viewed during the ceremony for all to see. You can include video clips, songs, images, etc. as long as you follow copyright laws."

More eye rolls. Of course, Mr. Horvik would say that. He's one of the writing teachers at our school and has told us all year to cite our sources.

"When I am done talking, please, find your group members. Lists are posted up on the front whiteboard. Then, send one person to the front to pick your famous quote out of this hat. Your one-to-two-minute video clips are due to me next week Wednesday. Please email your video clips so I can compile them into one incredible presentation. And remember, be creative and have fun! **Color outside the lines**! Let your creativity be your guide!"

*Whew, he's finally done talking!*

We all rush to the lists posted in the front of the classroom to find out who is in our group. Most of us have been in school together since kindergarten, so it's not a matter of knowing the people in our groups. It's just a matter of knowing which people we are grouped with.

"Lucy!"

"Luuucyyyyy!" Callie calls me from across the room.

I turn to answer, but my reply to Callie is interrupted by one 'hi,' one whispered 'hi,' and one awkward stare. Hayden, Nolan, and Elizabeth are in my group. Elizabeth gives me a quick head-to-toe look-over, then a smirk. "Nice shoes. They're so, **umm**, last year."

*Great, just what I needed. A diva with fashion sense, too.*

I search the room to find Callie and find her group in the back corner. We make eye contact from across the room, then she looks left and spots Elizabeth. Callie gives me a giant eye roll, then dramatically bows as if to mock Elizabeth's natural over-the-top ways. I give a quick laugh, then pull my attention back to my group.

Hayden, Elizabeth, Nolan, and I find a quiet spot at the end of the hallway outside of Mr. Horvik's classroom and start planning. Along with Elizabeth's natural tendency for diva-ness, she also had a way of taking charge and keeping our group on track.

No hellos or friendly greetings. Elizabeth starts with, "I already ran up to get our topic. We have 'Shine your light.' Everyone needs to come up with two ideas for the video. Let's meet tomorrow after school to plan. Be ready to discuss. Oh, and I am happy to do all the speaking parts," she adds.

And one more eye roll. But this time, it's from me.

"I think we know how to talk during a video, and any one of us can present, Elizabeth." Elizabeth actually sits silent for a minute as she stares back at Hayden. How Hayden can talk so calm and cool like that is beyond me.

Hayden turns to look at me and says, "Lucy, you don't mind presenting, right?"

"**Umm**, I think that sounds good. I mean greet. Great. I think that sounds great. Presenting would be, umm, foon. FUN!" *Get it together Lucy!*

Elizabeth's cell phone rings and thankfully pulls everyone's attention off of me. It gives me a much-needed moment to collect my thoughts. *Darn sweaty armpits!*

Elizabeth wastes no time telling us what to do as she hangs up her phone. "My ride's here. I have to get to a rehearsal for the latest show I am in. See you all tomorrow. Oh, and start to think about what we should wear in the video. You know, so we match." Elizabeth looks right at me with the same smug, know-it-all smile she used earlier.

"I have to go, too," said Hayden. "I have, **ummm**, soccer practice. Bye."

I wish Hayden didn't have to leave so soon. At least, he got **tongue-tied** leaving. I'm not the only one with an 'umm' in front of the group.

Our next meeting may be tomorrow, but I should have plenty of time tonight to balance my homework, softball practice, and time to brainstorm ideas for our 8th grade promotion ceremony video. I don't want to let down anyone in my group. Or hear any comments from Elizabeth.

With my group gone, I head to my usual after school spot by the art sculpture of hands reaching up, which was donated by a local artist. Nolan is already there waiting for me. *Geez, he's always so fast!*

"Nolan, ready to walk home with Callie and me?" He doesn't answer, but smiles. He almost always walks home with us since he moved into the neighborhood two years ago. Nolan doesn't walk to school with us because he still goes to before-school care. Nolan is quiet and lives in his own head a lot. Some kids make fun of him, but I've always found him to be really nice. I think Nolan likes to walk with us, even if he doesn't have much to say.

Nolan and I wait for Callie in silence, just watching the spring clouds overhead. Our wait drags on and on, and I notice I have **a pit in my stomach**. I'm not sure if it's from excitement about the end of the year, some nerves about creating the video presentation, or one too many smug smiles from Elizabeth.

## Social Thinking

People feel nervous in different situations. You may feel fine, but your friend may be a nervous wreck in the same situation. If someone says 'ummm' a lot, it could be a sign that he/she is feeling nervous or uncomfortable. Sometimes, people use 'ummm' because they are thinking of their words carefully. Or, they may be covering up a lie. 'Ummm' can have multiple meanings, so it is best to get to know the person or character who is talking. Do they always use 'ummm' and if so, why? Pay attention to how people and characters act with each other and in different places.

## Figurative Language

**Color outside the lines**: This expression is used to describe a situation with less rules and restrictions. Typically, when you color in a coloring book, you stay inside the lines. If you are told to color outside the lines, it means you can set your own rules. You are free to be creative and let your imagination take over and create what you want.

**Triple threat:** This is an expression used to describe someone who can act, sing, and dance (three talents). It is often used when talking about actors on stage, TV, or movies.

**Tongue-Tied:** This expression is used when someone is having a difficult time pronouncing words or finding the right words to say. They may be nervous (like Lucy), or just trying to put their words together. For example, "I was tongue-tied when I ran into my favorite professional basketball player at the coffee shop." This means one may be in so much shock seeing a famous person they can't get any words out.

**Pit in my stomach:** This is an expression used to describe an uncomfortable feeling in one's stomach. This can happen when you have a stomach bug, but it can also happen when you feel nervous or really upset about something.

# Chapter 3
# Crossing Lines

In true Callie form, she makes Nolan and I wait for a good fifteen minutes. I have to admit, the spring sunshine feels warm and wonderful on my face. Especially after being in school all day. Don't get me wrong, I love that my school is air-conditioned, but being outside with fresh air feels fantastic. Nolan waits quietly, looking from the clouds to watching a small chipmunk run back and forth out of the bushes. I wonder how Nolan stays so calm in his head all the time. Quiet times like this tend to make my brain work overtime.

*How could I have sounded so foolish? Just once, I want to be able to speak clearly without my racing heartbeat interrupting my brain. It's like my heart is so excited to get the words out that it takes over my mouth and it cannot possibly move as fast as my heartbeat. And don't even get me started on my sweaty armpits!"*

Wait up!" breaks through my thoughts. This is something I hear from Callie a million times a week.

"Hi, Cal! How did your group planning go?" I say with a fist bump handshake combo we always do.

I already know Callie will answer with 'fine,' but I sometimes wish other people also had totally embarrassing moments. Honestly, I don't want to use voodoo to harm anyone. It would just make me feel a little better to know that other kids have embarrassing moments, too. You know: A dropped cell phone in the hallway, an accidental fart that sneaks out during a class presentation, or spilled fruit punch on your new white jeans (Just for the record, only two of those three really happened to me).

"Our first meeting was great! I have Benny, Michael, Jefferson, and Anne in my group. They all talk really fast, but I think I can get them to slow down and listen to each other."

I guess fast talkers will do for now. Not exactly embarrassing, but at least they have things to work on as a group like the rest of us.

I always like my walk home. It is only twelve and a half minutes to my house from school, and Callie lives on a perfect diagonal from my house. If I look out the far-right corner of my front bedroom window, and Callie does the same in her living room, we can shine flashlights at each other. When we were younger, we thought we were so cool teaching ourselves Morse code. We started with S.O.S. Easy, right? Unfortunately, our neighbor, Mr. Theodore, is very knowledgeable and a veteran of the Vietnam War. He knows Morse code. He caught on to our flashlight codes from his front porch. What Callie and I thought was S.O.S. was in fact something totally different. Turns out, we were sending A.S.S. So much for that plan.

But that was years ago. We are mature 8th graders. And less than two weeks from being middle school graduates. I can't wait until we can showcase our video at the promotion ceremony which is right before the 8th grade formal dance. I'm so excited! Getting ready for this dance is the closest I will get to prom until, well, prom.

As Callie, Nolan, and I walk, I am silently planning my night. Pre-dinner (my mom calls it this because my snack is so big!), softball practice, math homework, revise my small moment writing assignment for literacy, and make time to brainstorm ideas for the video presentation.

"Cal, how am I supposed to plan a presentation about 'Shine your light' if I'm not 100% sure what that means, or what my group thinks this means?"

"I thought about that, too, for my own group. We have 'Every expert starts as a beginner.'" Then, in a bad British accent, Cal continues, "Just channel your inner wisdom. What does your soul think?"

I giggle a bit in my head. I love it when Callie gets philosophical.

"That's what all the famous people say when interviewed about movies or stage performances they are in. It's how they get into character and find the director's vision," Callie adds.

*Think, Lucy, think.* I'm searching deep down in my soul to find the answers I'm looking for, but a noise from behind brings me out of my head and back to reality. Then, a big rock hits my shoe and I feel anger shoot from my foot to my head. I spin around to give my best 'Knock it off or I'll tell Mom' speech to my little brother, but luckily I stopped before I started yelling. My little brother is not walking behind. It is just Nolan. Quiet Nolan. I calmed back down as quickly as the anger came. *Deep breath.*

I turn to him and ask, "Hey Nolan, what do you think about our topic for the presentation?"

Silence.

Pause.

Over Nolan's shoulder, I notice a figure running toward us: Long blonde hair moving side to side with each leaping step. Elizabeth is running through the crosswalk to catch up with us. Half out of breath, in an **overly dramatic way,** she hands Nolan and me each a small note with her fast handwriting penned across the paper.

"Here are

-gasp-

some quick reminders of

-gasp-

ways to prepare

-gasp-

-gasp-

for our group

-gasp-

video project."

"Elizabeth, I thought you left for your rehearsal?" I say, looking at her a bit confused.

Through her multiple gasps from 'running' so hard to catch up with us, she quickly tells me she had to stop at home to pick up her costume. Then she decided to scribble some notes for us, knowing she would pass by our street on her way to rehearsal.

I scan the list. Elizabeth watches me as if I might even make a mistake reading the list. There are bullet points with reminders such as: Write what 'Shine your light' means to you; practice saying your thoughts out loud into a mirror;

pay attention to your facial expressions; record yourself rehearsing on your cell phone; try saying your words with varying emotions (happy, sad, angry, scared, jealous, etc.); drink hot tea to keep your voice clear…

"Thanks, Elizabeth. You work fast," I say.

"Oh, it's just something I revised from a list I got from my drama coach at summer camp. I carry my drama notes with me at all times. You know. Just in case," Elizabeth shares without needing to gasp anymore.

For some reason, I don't think Elizabeth needs any hints or reminders when it comes to drama.

"Bye, Lucy!" And once again she is off.

Callie, Nolan, and I stand at the end of the crosswalk. We just look at each other. All a bit confused by what just happened. It's interesting how Elizabeth can be with us for 30 seconds and take complete control. How did she become the boss?

I look over at Callie to get a read on her take on what just happened. Callie has a big smile on her face. I can tell she is trying to hold in her laughter over the craziness known as Elizabeth. Callie starts mocking Elizabeth's voice and says,

"Just give yourself
*gasp*
3000 billion minutes
*gasp*
to work on this list.
*gasp*
And be sure to compliment me,
*gasp*
and tell me how great I am.

*gasp*…"

But she can't go on. Callie breaks down laughing.

"Callie, you are so funny." We laugh a bit more before we catch our breath. "But honestly, Elizabeth seems so bossy. And I am not going to miss my favorite show tonight just because I have to complete her checklist."

Callie agrees. I'm left with a happy heart. I am really lucky to live so close to my best friend. But today, what a twelve-and-a-half-minute walk. Talk about a **rollercoaster of emotions**. Like today. I went from having a pit in my stomach and feeling embarrassed from all of my 'ummms,' to laughing hysterically, to being reminded that I have the greatest best friend in the whole world.

"Bye, Callie. Bye, Nolan," I say, giving Callie one last fist bump for the day as we reach our street.

We say our good-byes and head up our driveways. My brain is still trying to search for ideas about 'Shine your light.' But for now, those ideas will have to wait. It's snack time, aka pre-dinner. It's amazing how hungry I get just by sitting and using my brain all day. 8th grade really zaps my energy and makes me hungry!


## Social Thinking

Pay attention to how group members act and treat each other. Elizabeth was gasping for air (well, not really; just being dramatic) and really bossy to others in her group. Elizabeth forgot to think about her group members, their feelings, and their ideas. She never gave others a chance to talk. She also made her presence known by gasping for air when she wasn't really that tired from running to catch up with Lucy, Nolan, and Callie. She may have been just looking for attention.

Also, watch for clues on how others respond. Nolan did not answer Lucy when she joined him at their after-school meeting spot and asked about his ideas. He just smiled. Lucy knows that Nolan does not say a lot. Lucy is using her social thinking skills and using what she knows about Nolan to interact respectfully with him. She wants Nolan to feel welcomed and safe. Lucy does not get mad at Nolan for being quiet. Instead, she continues to include him.

## Figurative Language

Lucy mentions that she has a rollercoaster of emotions. This expression means that she felt both highs and lows (happy to frustrated), just like a roller coaster goes up and down. Having feelings like this is perfectly normal unless the ups and downs get in the way of your daily life. If you find you have too many roller coaster moments, talk to a trusted friend or adult.

# Chapter 4
# Along the 'Write' Lines

While I love my twelve-and-a-half-minute walk home, I do not like my twelve-and-a-half-minute walk to school. I always feel more rushed in the morning than I do after school. My day starts with the usual: Get up, wash my face, make my bed, get dressed, fix my hair, eat (a lot – four bowls of Cheerios every day!), and brush my teeth. I rush out the door most days but end up waiting. Waiting for Callie. I love her dearly. She's a great best friend, but time management is not her strength. Not even a little. Not even the smallest bit.

*I'll wait one more minute.*
A minute passes.
*I'll wait one more minute.*
A minute passes.
*I'll wait one more minute...Oh, forget it. I'm leaving. I can't be late for school today.*

***Heart pounding***
***Heart pounding***
"LUUUCYYYYY!" Callie is running down her driveway, one shoe on, backpack in hand like a heavy kite,

and her favorite metal water bottle in the other (dented from the many times she dropped it running down the driveway and, in the halls, when late for class).

"Hi Cal. Can you ever be on time! Seriously, how can you live like this?"

"Like what?"

"Late! All the time!"

"Chill out, Lucy. We can just walk fast."

Thankfully, her long legs and my extra running at softball practice last night get us to school with a minute to spare. I never want to be late for any class, but especially Mrs. Jacobs's class. I love how she pushes me to be a better writer. And she never yells. Ever. Pretty amazing considering she deals with a bunch of hormonal, overly active teenagers all day long.

Mrs. Jacobs stands at the front of the room and directs us all to head up to our 'hot zone of learning' with our writing journals. We always start class up here. It's supposed to bring us together for 'an intense moment of quick learning before we go off on our own.' Unlike Callie, Mrs. Jacobs starts each lesson on time to respect our learning and work time.

"Today, we are going to push our conferencing partners to be better writers. But first, I want you to look at this quote I've projected. Read it to yourself. Write what it means to you. There will be time to share in two minutes go."

*Shoot. Can't see! Forgot my glasses at my seat.*

I squeeze, tiptoe, and stretch my way through the sea of students sitting on the floor, crammed together. Some writing quickly. Some are just staring at the screen in hopes that a grand idea will come into their heads if they stare long enough.

"Hey, watch it!"

Without even looking, I know that voice. It's Hayden's. He's sitting, holding his hand, then shaking it out. I can see the slight imprint from the sole of my tennis shoe on his hand. *Seriously, Lucy, can you do anything more embarrassing?*

'Sorry!' was all I could whisper before Mrs. Jacobs shouted out 'one more minute.'

Back at my table, I put my glasses on and speed-read the quote that was shared by Kay Moody. "If you want to be good at something, you must first be willing to be bad at it." I don't have time to go back to my seat. I quickly write my thoughts about this quote down in my journal.

*Work hard.

*Practice.

*Who's OK with being bad at something?

*Who's OK with mistakes?

*Why not just quit if you're bad?

I head back to my spot up front as Mrs. Jacobs gives the next set of directions. I am sure to take the longest way around the room, practically hugging the wall to avoid all hands- especially Hayden's.

We have to turn and share our ideas with our conferencing partner. I'm with Sarah. We just met this school year. She is super smart and can think of ideas in her head that no one else comes up with. I sometimes wonder if she gets the questions ahead of time so she can conduct extensive research before class starts. Her words always make perfect sense.

"What do you think?" Sarah asks.

I tell her my thoughts from my journal. Sarah nods and smiles politely. Besides being really smart, she is also very thoughtful. I don't think she has **a mean bone in her body.**

"Sarah, what do you think?"

"At first, I thought it meant we should try to be bad. But then I thought some more. Whenever we start something new, it's hard. It takes practice, time, and sometimes struggle before we get good at anything. It's the starting part we have to be OK with."

*Like I said, she always makes perfect sense.*

Mrs. Jacobs thanks us for sharing. She asks that while we read our writing partner's small moments and offer feedback. We need to give guidance that is helpful, not just say 'good' or 'fix this.' We are also reminded that this writing assignment may be personal since we are zooming in on a small moment in our own lives that shaped who we are today. Then, she directs us back to our seats.

Back at our table, Sarah and I exchange Chromebooks and start reading each other's work. Sometimes, I truly hate this part of the writing process. I never know what Sarah, or anyone for that matter, will think. I know Sarah is nice, but I worry that people will be too judgy. I look up at Sarah for her initial reaction to my writing. She looks distressed. *Is my work that bad? I mean, I was a bit rushed after softball practice, but how bad can it be? Oh my gosh – is Sarah sweating? Her face looks almost green!*

And faster than a mouse being chased by a cat, Sarah runs out of the classroom, grabbing the wastebasket with one fast swipe. She may be out of sight in the hallway, but the whole class hears her throw up not once, not twice, but three times. Giggles, groans of disgust, clapping, and one nasty comment about hot lunch covers up the sounds Sarah is creating in the hallway. Mrs. Jacobs jumps into action, quickly telling me to join table five to finish the feedback work before heading to the hallway. Table five? Yep, that would be Hayden's table. Happy dance in my head but I feel like a giant delivery of fear found its way to my **rapidly beating heart.**

I cautiously slide into the extra seat at Mario and Hayden's table. Hayden gives Mario a look as if to say, "You give her your paper to look at." Hayden and Mario have been friends for a long time. I think they can communicate just by looking at each other. From what I can see, the looks from Hayden are **filled with anger.** He must still be mad that I stepped on his hand. *Why did I have to be such a klutz?*

Mario smiles kindly and tells me to read Hayden's paper. I give Mario my Chromebook so he can give me feedback. *Hope my paper doesn't make him throw up, too.*

My heart speeds up again. Hayden's Chromebook is in front of me. I will be touching the same computer keys he used to type his paper. His skin cells left behind on the keyboard will stick to my fingertips.

*I may never wash my hands again.*

*Get back to work, Lucy,* a voice inside my head shouts at me. **Feedback**. That is what I need to provide. My rapid heartbeat falls back into rhythm as I read the first few lines of Hayden's paper. He wrote:

*I've eaten at the same dinner table my whole life. At first, I was in my high chair; then, my booster seat; but for the longest part of my life, I've sat in the chair between my younger sister, Elise, and my dad. At that table, we shared what we were thankful for before digging into each meal. Mom was a good cook, except for the fact that she used recipes with way too many vegetables.*

*My dinner table changed forever that Friday night. That first pizza night of March. Like always, we started dinner by sharing what we are grateful for, then we ate. This night felt different. Something was off. My parents sat in a weird silence, looking at each other, then warily at my sister and me. Mom was the first one to break the silence. "We love you both very much. That will never change. But after months of long talks, your father and I have run out of solutions. Your father and I are getting a divorce." From there, all I heard was static.*

I look up at Hayden. He catches my glance for a second, then buries his attention in Mario's Chromebook screen. My heart sinks as I read the rest of Hayden's paper. I can't believe I didn't see any of this coming. I now realize that when I sat down, Hayden was not still mad about me stepping on his hand. He was upset about me finding out his parents stepped on his heart. His family. His everything.

## Self-Regulation

**Rapidly beating heart:** We all need to pay attention to how we are feeling. Lucy's heart is beating rapidly. When someone is exercising or physically active, a fast heartbeat is expected. When someone is sitting in a class, this is less likely. Lucy is not addressing her unusually fast heartbeat.

It is likely stress. She should talk to or ask for help from a safe adult (ex: parent, teacher, etc.).

## Social Thinking

Lucy thinks Hayden is still mad at her for stepping on his hand at the start of class. Lucy needs to remember that not all situations are about her. People have their own thoughts and feelings. Sometimes, people get upset about something you did, but often, people have their own worries, anger, and sadness from situations you do not see or may never know about. Past and current experiences have a big impact on how someone acts. In this case, Hayden is upset by Lucy finding out about his parents' divorce.

Also, there are times when people get sick. It can be very embarrassing for the person who is not feeling well. Sarah did not feel well, and throwing up outside of her class was likely an experience she wishes never happened. The best thing to remember, if you are ever in this situation when someone is getting sick, is that if you can't say anything nice, don't say anything at all.

**Feedback:** Part of growing up is being able to provide feedback to others, and to also accept feedback from others. This is not always easy. You may worry about hurting someone's feelings. You may get not-so-good feedback on something that you feel is great just the way it is. You may feel angry if corrected. As hard as it may be, try to be open to feedback from others. We grow and strengthen our skills when we take time to learn and listen to others.

## Figurative Language

"I don't think she has a **mean bone in her body.**" This expression is used to describe someone who lives their life with kindness. Sarah's actions and words are so kind, it's as if she is not capable of being mean or rude. It is just not part of who she is.

# Chapter 5
# A Fine Line

Phy ed was a welcome distraction from writing class. I still feel like a jerk for thinking Hayden was mad at me. *Why does my brain do that?* He's dealing with so much, and all I manage to do is think he's holding on to anger toward me for stepping on his hand.

Mrs. Lacinski starts roll call as we enter the gym. "Roll call, please!" she yells.

"One!" from a low voice.

"Two!" from a high-pitched voice.

"Three!" from the other side of the gym.

My class has the fastest roll call in the entire school. Our teacher, Mrs. Lacinski, assigned each person a number on the first day of school. We shout out our numbers in order whenever she yells, "Roll call!" The faster we do this, the faster we get to the fun stuff.

"Four!" from the other side of the gym.

Pause.

Pause.

"Come on, Nolan, just shout it out!" is heard from a kid by the locker room.

I run over to Nolan and shout 'Five!' as he holds up his hand, showing all five fingers stretched high up in the air.

"Thanks," Nolan whispered to me.

"No problem, Nolan. Race you to the track?" **He may be quiet, but he is lightning fast**. Before I finish the word track, he is a mile ahead of me. I take off after him, leaving my worries from the writing class in my dust.

The air is warm for May and the sun has dried up most of the morning dew. The other gym classes are heading out to the track, too. Each class meets in their assigned spot outside on the track. Mrs. Lacinski reminds us that today we all have to run the mile. This is a test all students are required to do. For many students, it's the most dreaded day. But not me. I love this day! Not only do I get to run (which I love to do!), I also get to be with my best friend even though she's in the other phy ed class. After a few quick directions, my class is off and running.

I'm already a lap ahead when I catch up to Callie, running with Elizabeth. I slow down a bit and fall in pace behind them.

"So, did you like my practice tips last night? I know you overheard me talking to Lucy and Nolan."

Elizabeth always seems to have drama and acting on her mind.

"I did! I practiced for hours last night and used every tip you shared," Callie gushed.

"So glad I could help you. Maybe you could help me. What if Nolan joins your group, and Jefferson can come join my group? I think that would make the presentations way better. You know, based on height. You are the tallest in your group, and everyone in your group, except Jefferson, is tall. And, ummm, it's best to keep tall people together, don't you think?"

"Umm, sure…But don't you think Mr. Horvik will be mad if we switch?" Callie questions.

"Don't be so dramatic," Elizabeth explains. *Which is actually a really funny choice of words for her to use.* "If he asks, just say there was some confusion and Nolan went to the wrong group. You know, from all of his nerves."

"Seriously?" I say this a bit too loud as I invite myself to join in on their conversation. Elizabeth looks back long enough to catch my eye, then quickly runs off. *Funny how she managed to run and talk this time. She wasn't out of breath at all while talking to Callie…*

"Callie, you can't do that to your group! AND that's not fair to Nolan. You know, Mr. Horik probably put him with me since I'm one of the few people Nolan will even whisper to."

"Calm down, Lucy. It will be fine." Callie tries to convince me, but I don't want to hear any more. I'm so done with this conversation right now.

Callie continues to talk, but I just look down the track. I see Nolan cross the finish line. For the first time ever, I have no words for Callie. I race ahead, my feet carrying me as fast as they can, staying within the lines of my lane. I want to catch up with Nolan. My heart keeps beating faster and faster. But this time, it's not from running.

## Self-Regulation

Lucy said her heart is beating faster and faster, but not from running. She is really angry at Callie for agreeing with Elizabeth's plan to kick Nolan out of her group. Lucy thinks Nolan is not being treated fairly. In situations like this, Lucy needs to pay attention to how she is feeling. She can use her voice to stick up for her friends. This doesn't mean Lucy has to yell or be rude, but she has a right to stand up for Nolan and make sure he is being treated fairly.

## Social Thinking

Elizabeth seems to be planning a lot for the video presentation. She even says she wants to switch Nolan out of her group, without talking to Mr. Horvik, because of Nolan's height. This doesn't make any sense. Nolan's height should not matter when making a video presentation. Sometimes, people act selfishly and try to get their own way. To do this, they tell lies or stretch the truth. Elizabeth should think about how Nolan, and the group, might feel about being kicked out of the group.

## Strengths

Nolan is described as lightning fast (this expression means he can run really fast). It can be easy to focus on differences to describe someone, like Nolan, who does not talk much. But Lucy can see beyond this. She knows he is more than just someone who is really quiet. She can see Nolan for his strengths such as his ability to run fast and his kindness toward others.

# Chapter 6
# Battle Lines

So, phy ed was not as great as I hoped, even though the sun was shining and I got to run. I just need to forget about Callie for now and focus on my classes.

*Positive thoughts, Lucy.*

My day does actually get better…until science. Well, it isn't actually in science class. It is what happens that night BECAUSE of science class. It is because of my required homework that night for science class that things get even messier for me. I have to study for my final unit test on astronomy, and I need some note cards. This should be a very simple problem to solve. It is not.

After school, I start my homework once my pre-dinner is finished, just like I do most nights. I have everything I need to study for my test except note cards.

"Hey, Levi! Can I have some note cards? Levi, Leeeeevi!" No answer. *Great. Now I have to get up and get them myself. And I just got comfortable in my chair.*

Entering Levi's room is like entering a video game. The floor is covered with every type of LEGO creation invented. There's a castle for his action figures, stuffed animals, and board games. All his favorite treasures are out, forming a maze-like pattern on the blue carpeting below my feet. Levi is careful to keep everything where he wants it to be kept. If anything is out of place, the maze turns into a dead end.

I carefully make my way to his desk, narrowly avoiding a LEGO spaceship that attacks my pinky toe with the smallest, pointiest piece sticking out of the corner.

Like his room floor, his desk is arranged with everything in its place. Pencils in the cup holder with pointed tips facing down, Chromebook perfectly centered and charging, and his iPhone charging…wait. With my phone charger. *Ugh, seriously!*

"MOOOOM! Levi took my charger again!"

Mom is surprised to find me in Levi's room, but asks what I need.

"Mom! Levi took my charger again. I'm so sick of him taking my stuff. He's such a brat!"

My mom gives me that look like *I'm going to take a minute to pause before I speak.*

With a slight sigh, my mom replies, **"Lucy, your scream for help made me think something was seriously wrong.** Your brother taking your charger without permission is not considered an emergency. I'm guessing you used your extra charger anyway last night. Why are you in his room in the first place?"

"Mom, I need note cards. I have a huge science test to study for. This is important."

"Just to be clear," Mom started. "You are mad at Levi for going into your room and taking something without permission, **yet you are doing the exact same thing** by being in Levi's room and taking note cards, correct?"

"Sure Mom, take his side. You always do. Fine. You want me to just leave the note cards here and fail the test. Great."

And with that, I storm out of Levi's room. Only this time, my pinky toe is less forgiving. It clips the same corner of the LEGO spaceship, but this time it takes down the entire creation, causing it to crash into hundreds of little pieces as it hits the side of the nightstand. It happened so fast. There was no chance to try and catch it. I hear my mom call my name as I leave. But I just keep walking to my room. My only response is the **slamming of my door.**

## Social Thinking:

Lucy is struggling to see this situation from another point of view. Her mom sees this situation and how it impacts Levi. Lucy is mad that her brother took something of hers without permission, yet she is doing the exact same thing to her brother (went into his room/took note cards). She is mad at her brother but not at herself. Lucy forgot to use her social thinking. It is unexpected for Lucy to be mad at Levi, yet think it is OK for her to do the same thing. Lucy should treat her brother the way she would like to be treated.

Size of the problem: Lucy's mom said, **"Lucy, your scream for help made me think something was seriously wrong."** Lucy forgot to think about the size of the problem. No one was seriously hurt or injured. Lucy's charger is in her brother's room, safe and not damaged. And in a short while, the problem of Levi having her charger will not matter. It's OK for Lucy to question why her charger was in

Levi's room, but she could have talked it through with Levi or her mom, without yelling and screaming.

## Body Language

Lucy is upset. Besides breaking Levi's LEGO creation and yelling at her mom, she slammed her bedroom door. Lucy was trying to make a point and let others know she was angry, but everyone around her already knew she was upset. Lucy needs to find ways to manage her anger and deal with her feelings without yelling or slamming doors. One suggestion would be to talk with her mom or let her mom know she needs a few minutes to take a break.

# Chapter 7
# Rewriting the Lines

I flop onto my bed and remain motionless for the next fifteen minutes. At first, my head was pounding with anger. **My rapid heartbeat** is fueling my brain with stress. But as time passes, my breathing slows down. The anger in my fists relaxes. My jaw is not clenched anymore. My breathing slows back down to normal.

Finally, I lay in stillness. My heart beat calmly again. Unfortunately, now the replay of what just happened in my brother's room is slowly sinking in. I am now starting to understand how bad things got. I am now starting to see how I overreacted. I am sad but also mad at myself for letting my emotions take over like this. I wish I could hit pause and just stay in the safety and calm of my room. But like all good things, this feeling doesn't last long.

Suddenly, my bedroom door swings open and hits the wall behind it. I nearly jumped off the bed. My legs jerked to the side of my bed into a standing position. The strong force on the other side of the door can only be caused by one thing: A very angry ten-year-old. This angry version of my younger brother is standing in front of me with his fists tightly closed, chest rising as he breathes fast, face red, and eyes darting directly at me. I think there are even lines down his cheeks that show the path where each tear fell.

"You broke my LEGO spaceship! Do you know how long it took me to make that? And stay out of my room! You messed up my desk and my note cards are missing!"

And in no time, my anger is back.

"Seriously, Levi! YOU took my charger! Stay out of MY room!"

"No, I didn't. I did NOT go into your room, and I did NOT take your charger!"

"Whatever, Levi. I saw it on your desk and took it back. I know it's mine because it is pink AND has my initials on it, see?" I toss the charger toward his head, narrowly missing him. But, my charger hits something else. An unintentional target.

"What the – ouch!"

Unfortunately, I know that voice too well. It's my mom.

In a voice louder and higher pitched than normal, the words come out fast. "You two better figure this out quick! I should be able to walk in this house without a charger, or anything for that matter, hitting me in the face."

Levi and I race to say 'he/she started it' with fingers pointing at the other, but my mom pulls the parent card.

"ENOUGH! I would like to come home from a long day at work and enjoy my family without having to be a referee. This is ridiculous! You two have three minutes to figure this out civilly, or I'm taking all devices. If you can't show kindness to actual people in front of you, I have no guarantee you will be kind to someone online or on social media or anyone who is on the other side of your screen."

"But…" in unison comes from Levi and me. Mom cuts off our words with a single hand raised in protest.

"Your time starts now!" and Mom heads back to the kitchen without another glance at either of us.

One minute passes. Levi and I glare at each other with no words to exchange. Heavy sighs, but no words.

*I will not lose my phone because of some stupid note cards I borrowed from my stupid brother.*

"Fine! Levi. I'll apologize, but only because I have to," I say.

"Not because you have to. It's because you need to. You broke my spaceship and messed up my desk!"

"Well, you took my charger. STAY OUT of my room!"

"I didn't take your charger!"

Just then, Dad is back from work and standing in the doorway. He looks like he had a rough day; his tie is loose and the top buttons of his shirt are open. Dad asks Levi to leave. Without a hello, my dad is pulled into this mess.

"UGH, see! You and Mom do favor Levi!" I yell out to my dad so Levi can hear as he leaves. My dad stands quietly for a minute. *This is not going to end well.*

I can tell Dad is trying to be calm despite the fact that this is probably not what he wants to deal with when he steps in the door. He sits on the side of my bed and starts talking calmly. "Lucy, I heard you are mad at Levi for taking your charger. He didn't do it. I did. I lent it to him. He left his at Grandma's house. I texted you so you would know. Didn't you read my text?"

"I didn't get a text, and no, I don't read texts, Dad. That's so yesterday. Everyone snaps (aka Snapchats)."

"Lucy, check your phone. And it's not so yesterday. Your behavior, on the other hand, is. It's OK to feel angry, but your reaction is way over the top. No one is seriously injured, no one has died. Use your words." Dad pauses and waits to see what I will do.

*Ugh, I hate the 'use your words talk!'*

I grab my phone and scroll through my texts. And there it is: 7:48 PM. **Dad must have sent it when I was still at softball practice.**

*Well, this isn't good.*

## Self-Regulation

Lucy knows her heart is beating fast. She is angry and feels everyone is against her. Lucy could have asked for some time to regroup and try some calming strategies before talking with anyone. This is important because Lucy's problem/situation is a small problem. It will not matter in a day or two. She is acting as if there is a BIG problem (ex: Someone was in a car accident, someone is sick in the hospital, etc.). Lucy needs to remember to stop, look at a situation, and match her reaction to the size of the problem.

## Social Thinking

When upset, it can be difficult to see another person's point of view or idea. Lucy did not listen to Levi when he told the truth, and she didn't believe her dad at first. Lucy should have taken time to listen instead of trying to hold on to her anger. She could have avoided the situation of hitting her mom when she threw the charger (another decision Lucy should have changed) if she would have listened to her brother. Lucy needs to consider the size of the problem and how to self-regulate when she is getting upset.

## Fixing a Problem

Lucy yelled at her brother, broke her brother's Lego project, yelled at her dad, and hit her mom with a phone charger. Lucy needs to think about positive ways to rebuild her relationship with everyone. This means she needs to own her behavior (*we own ALL our behavior: good and bad), and think of other ways to handle frustrating situations.

# Chapter 8
# Clearing the Lines

Dinner is awkward. Mom and Dad chat about their day and ask Levi about his. I get the usual 'What did you learn about today?' and 'What homework do you have?' but I don't feel like talking. Levi finishes his dinner first, puts his dishes in the dishwasher, and is off to change into his uniform for his baseball game. This leaves just me, Mom, and Dad at the table.

*#Awkward.*

Mom and Dad pause after he leaves and give me that 'how are you going to fix this' look. I know this situation isn't going to get any better if I just sit here. I might as well get this over with.

"I'm sorry I freaked out about my charger, and that I yelled at Levi. And that his spaceship broke. And Mom, I'm sorry the charger hit you on the head." I say this all fast and with little expression. My words are now out and sounded like an apology, but my tone sounded more like I'm still annoyed.

My mom adds, "And?"

That's the thing with my parents. Everything is a long talk. They say an apology should have three parts: State what you are sorry for; state what can be expected in the future; and state how to fix what was wronged.

I try once again. "I will use my words to explain why I am upset instead of freaking out, and I will go help Levi rebuild his spaceship." But then I kept talking. It's like my mind and mouth are on automatic pilot and I can't stop my words from turning into a train wreck. "But Dad, this is your fault. You should have told me you took my charger!" *And there it is.* **Why can't I just say I'm sorry!** *Why do I have to keep flapping my mouth?*

"I did. I texted you because you were at practice," Dad answers, but I can hear a bit of frustration in his voice.

"No one reads texts, Dad."

"How many of Callie's texts have you missed?"

"None," I quickly answered. Maybe a little too quickly.

"Fine. I get it." My voice is starting to sound calmer. More like the real me again. Likely a sign of defeat. *Time to stop arguing.* " I'll read texts from you, and I will talk to you or Mom when I need something instead of just taking it." We sit in silence for another moment.

My parents make the next move and come over and give me a hug. I act like I'm annoyed by this, but actually, I'm a bit relieved. My parents thank me for my plan to fix things and handle situations better.

Our moment of peacefulness is interrupted by the loud ring of the doorbell.

"I'll get it!" is heard as Levi streaks past us in a blur to open the door. It's Nolan. He hands Levi a video game. They always swap games. Levi jumps for joy and does a little happy dance at the sight of this video game.

"Hi, Nolan," I say as I walk over to greet him in the doorway. He waves back to me, smiles at Levi, then turns to head home. And Levi is once again a blur. He wants to sneak in a few minutes of video gaming before heading off to his baseball game.

"Don't take too long, Levi. Leaving in five," Dad shouts upstairs.

I decide to stay in the kitchen to help with the dishes. It's one way for me to show my parents that I am sorry for how I acted. *Sometimes, I just don't know why I get so angry.*

## Social Thinking

### *Why can't I just say I'm sorry!*

Your words matter. You need to think about people and their ideas just as they think about you and your ideas. Lucy made a mistake. It is better to acknowledge the problem, and find a way to make it right. Because no matter what, Lucy (as well as you, me…everyone) has to own her behavior, both the good and the bad. Lucy needs to make right what was wrong. It can be hard to admit when you make a mistake. Everyone has moments like this when one feels angry over something little. Part of growing up knowing it is OK to admit you were wrong or made a mistake. Growing up is about learning from mistakes and taking ownership of what you say and do.

# Chapter 9
# A Direct Line to The Moon

Besides the fact that Callie is actually on time this morning, shocker, my day is off to a good start. With all of the drama from last night at home, I've forgotten about my anger toward Callie as we start our walk to school. Actually, we don't even talk about the 8th grade promotion ceremony project. We just walk to school talking about lunch, who likes who, and what we are wearing to the 8th grade dance. The important stuff.

Writing class, phy ed, and math are smooth sailing. Honestly, it's been one of those days when things are going as expected. At least for the first part of the day, I feel calm. But sometimes I worry when everything is going well. Like, I'm waiting for the next bad thing to happen because nothing goes well forever.

In the halls, everyone is in a good mood today. Maybe it is the end-of-the-school-year-highs or the news about Mrs. Aide's frogs escaping the science lab last night. This has students laughing and extra loud in the halls. Everyone seems to have a story about how they were the ones who helped corral the frogs back. It's funny listening to the stories because I could have sworn there were only two frogs in the tank, but as the stories have made their way from student to student, I think I've heard there were up to 50 frogs on the loose running, well…hopping, through the school! I guess this is a perfect example of the game telephone. The original message starts one way and gets turned into something completely different as it is passed along.

Despite epic tales from 'The Day the Frogs Got Loose,' walking into science class does not feel light or funny. Something feels different. I'm not as excited as everyone around me. Not sure if it is the test today, or the memory of Levi's LEGO spaceship breaking into pieces (triggered by the sounds of someone's pencil case dropping in the hallway and scattering pencils everywhere. Zip your case people!). Or maybe I didn't sleep as well as I thought I did last night. Maybe I'm just starting to feel tired. No matter the cause, I just feel weird the moment I walk into science. My **heart is beating a bit faster. Must just be my nerves**.

Our science tests are always done on paper. We can use two note cards with our own notes to help our thinking. Mrs. Aide separates the tables on test days and asks that we pile our supplies in the center of the tables to form a privacy screen. Callie is across from me. She always sets her pile just off center so she can make faces at me during tests.

I spot Nolan at the next table over, searching through his pencil case, his pockets, a binder, and repeating the process again. Each time he searches, he is looking around faster and more frantically. *He must not have a pencil.* I quickly grab one of mine and walk over to his table. As I set the pencil in front of him, he looks right up at me with his teary eyes. He doesn't say anything, but his shoulders relax, and I hear a slight sigh of relief.

Back at my seat, Mrs. Aide is passing out our tests. She looks at me with a smile and nod. She must have watched me give Nolan a pencil.

"Class, before you begin, please, write your first and last name at the top. Read the prompt carefully. Be sure to include enough information for each prompt to show me your understanding of the science concepts being assessed. When you are finished, come up to the front lab table, and staple your notecards to the top of your test. Your work goes in this basket here. You may read quietly at your seat until class is dismissed."

Teachers always give the same directions on each test and repeat them each time, even though we have heard them a thousand times! Must be a requirement to be a teacher. *Focus Lucy. Time to get this test over with.*

I add my first and last names to the top and read the prompt through twice. "The moon has no source of light. Explain how we are able to see the moon on Earth. Then, how can we apply this thinking to ourselves?"

*Wait – what?*

*Am I reading this right? I have to compare the moon's light to myself!*

Heartbeat.

Heartbeat.

After five minutes of staring at my test prompts, the sound of Elizabeth sneezing her overly dramatic, high-pitched sneeze brings me back to reality. I reread the prompt again, and my brain is finally ready to work. Thankfully, I wrote about how the moon reflects light on my note card last night. Well, actually, thanks to Levi I have a note card with the right science information. Once I start writing my answer, I don't even really need to read the information on my note card because I remember what I wrote. **My pencil starts moving quickly across the paper, adding clever astronomy words as it goes,** such as: Reflected light, fully illuminated, moon's trajectory, and orbit. But then, my pencil stops to pause. I am not sure how to answer the part about how the moon reflecting light is like me.

*OK, Lucy. Think. Think. Think. Ideas. Moonlight. Me. Shine. Sunlight. Shine. Reflect. Shine.* But instead of answering the prompt for this assessment, an idea pops into my head. I know what to do for my group's video for the 8th grade promotion ceremony!

## Self-Regulation

Lucy's heart is beating faster again. She is feeling weird yet doesn't do anything about it. Like Lucy, we all need to pay attention to how we are feeling. If we feel weird or upset, we can take some calming breaths, ask for help, take a break, talk to a safe adult, or find a friend. Even taking a moment with three slow, deep breaths has been scientifically proven to change your brain chemistry and calm your mind. Try it. It really works!

## Figurative Language

**My pencil starts moving quickly across the paper, adding clever astronomy words as it goes** is a form of personification. Lucy's pencil is given human qualities in this sentence. Her pencil is not actually writing ideas, she is the one coming up with the ideas.

# Chapter 10
# Hook, Line, and Sinker

I did it! My final science test of the year is finished. The hallway after class is busy with students rushing to their next class. My timing is perfect. I have a great idea for our video, and, as if planned by the universe, Elizabeth walks by just as I step into the busy stream of students crowding the halls.

"Elizabeth! Wait up!" I say as I pick up my pace to catch up next to her. She stops and waits for me. In fact, she actually seems to be in a good mood.

We stand like an island in the busy hallway. Lines of students heading in opposite directions are on either side, but we just stand in the middle while others try to get by around us. "I have an idea…" is all I manage to get out.

Just when I think Elizabeth may actually listen to me, she smiles and boldly interrupts me mid-sentence. For some reason (*again!*), I can't find my words to utter anything. Instead, I just find myself reaching out my hand as she holds out a packet of pages for me.

"I have written the script for our presentation! Isn't that great!"

Elizabeth is wide-eyed and smiling as she stands before me. She pauses and waits for me to react, like she is hoping I will return the same excitement for HER ideas.

"**Ummm**" is all I manage to get out.

Unaware of my feelings, Elizabeth continues, "And Nolan asked to be with Callie. Isn't that great! Everything is great! I can't stop saying 'GREAT!'"

"But Nolan is in our group." *Finally! Something comes out of my mouth. My voice is not as strong as I would like it to be, but it's better than nothing.*

**"Don't be so emotional, Lucy. You know, it would be impossible for Nolan to be with us since he is so qui…I mean, tall. And besides, Callie totally begged me to let Nolan be in her group**. They are doing something about starting as a beginner, then taking giant steps into the future. Since they are all tall, they are the giants. Bye!"

Once again, I am left speechless. This is getting a bit ridiculous. Does she not know I heard her entire conversation on the track with Callie? *Guess not.* But that does remind me that Callie totally went along with Elizabeth's plan to trade Nolan out of my group! Elizabeth is always so busy planning that she can't manage ever paying attention to any ideas but her own. And now, she pulled Callie into her selfishness. Elizabeth is long gone, in the stream of students heading to class. I stand in the middle by myself, still speechless.

"Luuucyyyyy! Wait up!"

I know that call anywhere. It's Callie. My feet are not sure if they should move forward through the hall to my next class, or stop and wait as commanded from behind. Honestly, I don't know who to be madder at: Callie or

Elizabeth. I think Callie fell under Elizabeth's spell. It is time for me to **find my voice**, but it's not for my own needs this time. I need to find my voice to stand up for Nolan.

For now, my feet decide to move forward. I pretend I don't hear Callie, and join the stream of students walking to their next destination.

## Social Thinking

Elizabeth is not thinking about Nolan or his feelings. She is only thinking of herself. It seems like Elizabeth doesn't like the fact that Nolan is so quiet, but she doesn't want to appear rude (even though she is most of the time). She made up a lie about him needing to join the other group because he was tall. Elizabeth blames Lucy for being **so emotional**. Elizabeth is using this strategy to take the focus away from the lie she is telling and to place guilt on Lucy. Lucy was emotional because she knew what Elizabeth was doing was not right. Lucy needs to find ways to use her words and stand up for Nolan. This can be very difficult. Especially since Elizabeth has a strong personality and appears comfortable, or unaware, of her constant rudeness. If Lucy feels overwhelmed, like she does in this situation, she should speak up or ask for help from a trusted friend or adult.

## Figurative Language

**Find my voice** is an expression used to describe a time when you need to say something, but the words do not come fast enough. Lucy has the ability to speak. She does not have laryngitis. Unfortunately for Lucy, she is intimidated by

Elizabeth's rudeness and power. She becomes scared and shuts down. Lucy needs strategies to help her communicate her frustrations so she can think, find words to express her thoughts, and talk to Elizabeth. Lucy does not need to be rude back to Elizabeth. Firmly speaking her truth with kindness can be more powerful than yelling insults.

# Chapter 11
# Hardline

The weather feels like summer as I head outside after school. And it's Thursday. Callie and I have a standing agreement to walk to the local coffee shop after school every Thursday. Nolan meets with a group at the local community center on Thursdays, so it's just the two of us. We don't really like coffee, but they make fancy, fruity drinks and the best chocolate chip cookies.

We aren't the only ones who had the idea to head there for a treat. Eleven people are in line ahead of us. Many look like they snuck out of their office for some fresh air and sunshine. I need some sunshine right now. *And I'm hangry. Can this line move any faster?* I look over at Callie. The little voice in my head is growing more and more angry with her. I keep thinking about what Callie said on the track the other day, and how Elizabeth treated me in the hallway earlier today. Heartbeat is picking up.

"So then I told Sarah…" Callie went on.

"Callie. Stop!"

**"Geez, what's got you so cranky?"**

**"You!" I say a little too loud.** Three or four people in front of us stare back at me. I know I have to confront Callie. She can't let Elizabeth take over every situation. Actually,

I need to take my own advice and confront Elizabeth, too. She has no right to take over our entire final project for the 8th grade promotion ceremony without talking to the group first.

"Callie, I heard you talking with Elizabeth on the track in phy ed the other day. And today, Elizabeth told me how she kicked Nolan out of the group because of his height. Seriously! How could you let her kick Nolan out of my video project group?"

Callie looks at me for a moment.

No words.

Just stares.

It's hard to tell if she is mad at me or upset she got caught. She is the first to break the silence.

"Lucy, I only agreed to do the switch because Nolan is my friend. If Elizabeth is going to kick him out, I don't want him to end up in some random group."

"But how is that fair to Nolan? Doesn't he deserve a say?" I added.

The line at the coffee shop is moving faster now. Only two people ahead of us. I walk forward. I need a minute to think. I walk forward and I'm not quite as mad at Callie now, knowing she was just trying to protect Nolan.

"Sorry, Cal. I guess I should not have assumed you were just trying to get on Elizabeth's good side."

"Good side? Pa-lease! That girl is so dramatic. She never lets anyone get a word in. If I had my way, I'd pull all of you over to my group for the presentation."

*Pause.*

"Wait. Pull over the whole group?"

And with that, a grand idea pops into my head. "Callie, is your group really doing something about starting as a beginner and giants?"

"Starting as a beginner, yes. Giants, no."

"Cal, what if we did combine groups? Do you think the rest of your team would agree? I have an idea that involves the moon, and your idea about starting as a beginner. It will work perfectly. Our topics fit together like…peanut butter and jelly. Like hamburgers and fries. Like movies and popcorn. Like…"

"Geez, OK. I get it. And we need to get you some food. You clearly have food-brain right now," Callie says with a smile.

"And we could even bring in the idea of giants."

"No need. That thing about giants is only in Elizabeth's head. Let's not go there. Leave the giants in Elizabeth's head and let it go."

Then, Callie starts humming the theme song from 'Frozen.' Callie may not have been in the hallway with me when Elizabeth handed me the script, but she knows exactly what I am referring to when it comes to Elizabeth. I guess that is just one of the many benefits of a BFF.

Finally, we make it to the front of the line. My stomach growls as I'm searching for my pre-dinner in the display case of chocolatey cupcakes, fruity muffins, and delicious homemade sandwiches. After we place our order, we find a seat so we can get right to work on what Callie has now named, Operation Combination. Callie is in charge of sending a Snapchat message to everyone in both of our groups. I am in charge of emailing Mr. Horvik and Elizabeth about the plan to combine groups.

"In the words of Elizabeth, this is going to be GREAT!" I joke.

Cue the eye roll from Callie.

## Social Thinking

Lucy found her words when talking with Callie. She stood up for Nolan. Despite this, there is still a social misunderstanding. Lucy forgot that Callie respects Nolan as much as she does. This misunderstanding caused a lot of frustration for Lucy. When dealing with Elizabeth, Callie had a different approach to standing up to Elizabeth. Callie didn't get tongue tied, yell, demand, or take over the situation. Instead, Callie just made sure Nolan was included. Lucy felt relieved to know that Callie was looking out for Nolan. Talking through her frustration was a positive choice.

It can be tough to talk calmly with others when you are upset. Lucy likely stood up for Nolan when talking to Callie, instead of Elizabeth, because they are best friends. Either way, Lucy is starting to use her voice to help others. This is a positive sign of growth and maturity.

# Chapter 12
# Crossing the Line

After dinner with my family, my Snapchat is blowing up. Callie wasted no time reaching out to both project groups. Despite always being late, Callie did a great job connecting with everyone right away. I have not had a chance to email Mr. Horvik yet. Luckily, almost everyone in both groups is on board and likes my idea of combining our groups. There is only resistance from one. Elizabeth.

"Way too many people in this group!" – Elizabeth.

"It will be fun! The more the merrier, right?" – Callie.

"Running out of time. Let's get this done." – Michael.

"Too busy. I'll let Mr. Horvik know. No hard feelings. Gotta get to my rehearsal. **b4n**." – Elizabeth.

"Elizabeth, just stay." – Lucy.

…no response

"Group meeting tomorrow after school. Bring ideas and let's record our video!" – Callie.

Later that night, I get a message directly from Elizabeth.

"Lucy, I emailed Mr. Horvik and told him about the groups coming together. I simply do not have time to meet and create the presentation. Good luck with your group video!"

"Thanks, Elizabeth. See you tomorrow."

I guess it is settled. Even though she can drive me crazy, I do feel bad that Elizabeth dropped out. But now we all have a chance to actually be in the video and have speaking roles. And we can all share ideas. And Nolan won't have to deal with moving groups. **I guess it will all be fine.**

## Social Thinking

**I guess it will all be fine.**

Lucy has mixed feelings. On one side, Lucy knows that when working in a group, it is important to let everyone have a chance to share ideas. This can be difficult for some people, like Elizabeth, who like to have everything their way (control). Elizabeth is not a helpful group member. She does not use her social thinking when talking to people. Elizabeth needs to remember that just like she has ideas, so do others. In any social situation, some people may like your ideas, others may not. Being part of a group often requires people to listen and compromise. On the other side, Lucy knows it is important to include everyone, so she feels bad Elizabeth dropped out of the project.

Texting Language: **B4n** means, "Bye for now."

# Chapter 13
# Writing the Lines

After what feels like the longest school day ever, my group meets after school to plan our presentation. I'm so excited! Callie decided the coffee shop was the best place to meet. The shop is a bit distracting with people coming and going, but it also offers the best treats – brain food! I wave at Michael, Hayden, and Benny, who are already there when we arrive. They are eating what looks like enough food for ten people!

I jump in line before the rest of my group gets here so I can beat the rush. Waiting in line also gives me time to think back about my day. At school, Elizabeth was actually, well, nice. She was friendly and didn't seem upset. She even complimented my outfit today. Who knew she liked softball tournament t-shirts from last summer. I guess she really is just really busy with her other rehearsals. Maybe with the stress of this presentation gone, she is actually pleasant to be around.

"Lucy! Over here!"

Callie is waving her arms in the back corner as if her loud voice was not enough to get my attention. *That's Callie for you.*

At the back corner of the coffee shop, there is enough seating for everyone. They had to pull three small tables to make room for all eight of us, but everyone has a chair. A voice. A place in this group.

Callie raises her lemonade as a symbol of 'cheers!' to get us started. I think she is happy to take the lead. At least, she does it in a respectful, non-bossy way.

"Thank you, everyone, for coming. Combining our two groups was Lucy's idea. Lucy, can you explain your idea?"

"Sure!" I say. I look around at this great group of people and stop when I see Hayden.

Heart beating faster.

*Just take a deep breath and start talking.*

"I thought of an idea after taking our final science test. We had to write about how the moon reflects light, and our group was assigned the phrase, 'Shine your light.' The rest of you were given, 'The expert was once a beginner.' This made me think about how we view and treat others. Our light can be bright and help those around us, or we can keep it to ourselves and force others to stand in our shadows. When we shine our own light, we can help ourselves and others. We need to shine our light bright and let others shine their light, too. We need to remember that everyone has their own talents, strengths, and things to work on. When you meet someone who is struggling, shine your light to help them."

I can't believe it. My words are coming out clearly. I've even managed to look at Hayden without getting **tongue**

**tied**. For the first time in my life, I really believe in what I'm doing.

"Lucy, I like your idea. I can help put all the video clips into a movie. But what will this video look like?" Michael asks.

"I have an idea," Jefferson shares. "What if we each use the flashlight on our phones to shine light on ourselves when we talk? Then, we can shine our light on the next person who is going to speak. It would be like we are passing our light, but also our words."

"Nolan, what do you think about this idea?" Hayden asks.

Nolan smiles, then looks over at Michael, sitting next to him. He shares, using a really quiet voice, "Michael, I can help you make the movie on the computer."

Michael nods and gives Nolan a fist bump.

It's funny how a 1–2 minutes video clip can take so long. I guess laughing hysterically between each video-take slows down the recording process. First, Callie starts laughing after taking a sip of her fancy lemonade from the coffee shop. She laughs so hard; it comes out of her nose! Even Nolan notices. We all laugh until our stomachs hurt.

After five minutes of trying to control our laughter and tears (which I might add makes it even harder to stop laughing), Jefferson calms down enough to start recording again. Jefferson tries to say, "Shine your light to help others be bright," but he jumbles his words and says, "shine your bright to help others bite." Cue more uncontrollable laughter.

Then, Callie starts to laugh and accidentally spits out her drink on me! I'm starting to think Callie should not have any beverage close by while doing any work. Customers look over at us multiple times. Some look annoyed. But some seem to smile when they notice we are working on a project.

My heart isn't racing. I just feel happy.

Michael and Nolan are amazing at editing our video quickly. In less than 20 minutes, they download all of the video clips from our phones and manage to edit, connect, and compile our random videos into an Oscar-worthy, award-winning video. Watching our completed video gives me goosebumps. I pause to look around at the others who all came together to create this video. Faces smiling; people talking with one another; everyone helping to clean up the space we took over in the coffee shop.

Happy heartbeat.

Happy heartbeat.

Our video is a powerful example of what can happen when people work together. And I can't wait to see it projected at our 8th grade promotion ceremony!


## Social Thinking

Lucy and her friends work well together. They share ideas, listen to each other, and are open to the idea of working together to finish a common goal. When groups work together like this, people are often more willing to take risks and share ideas. And honestly, working with group members who use social thinking is more fun!

Group members have a responsibility to make sure all are included. Notice how people who are quiet, like Nolan, were pulled into the group with questions, and given a chance to help. Michael's gesture of a fist bump was another way to show inclusion and support. When you work with others, think about how you act. Are you the vocal one with ideas? If yes, be open to listening to ideas from others too, even if they are not exactly like yours. Are you the quiet one? If yes, be open to asking questions if you are unsure what to do. Are you the one who is a good listener? If yes, include others by asking questions and complimenting others. Share your ideas, too. Are you the one who is restless and needs to move around? If yes, ask to get supplies, help with parts of the task that are hands-on, or grab a fidget to help you focus on the task.

# Chapter 14
# Drop a Line

Callie, Nolan, and I have the best walk home from the coffee shop. Nolan is exceptionally smiley, too. It seems he liked making the video as much as we did. He even started our video by whispering 'Shine your light' and ended the video with 'All experts start out as beginners. Shine your light to all.'

I still can't believe Elizabeth tried to pawn Nolan off to some other group! Who cares if he doesn't talk much. Who cares if he is not as dramatic as Elizabeth. Who cares if he only does well when given helpful directions. I think Nolan did great! He even used a fun accent. He sounded like a voice-over actor that could be used in a movie trailer for the next summer blockbuster.

"Nolan, you did great!" Callie chimes in.

Nolan smiles even bigger. I hope the three of us still get to walk home from high school together. Everyone says things change when you start high school: New classes, new friends, new routines. I guess Callie and I have made it this far in life together. Hopefully, we will stick together until we cross the finish line (aka high school graduation).

We relive the funny moments from recording our project: Mispronounced words, when Callie shot her drink out of her nose, and when she spilled her drink on me. We laugh and laugh until Callie suddenly stops. You can always tell when an idea pops into her head. She will stop whatever she is doing, actually gets quiet. Really quiet. And stares off as if she sees the new idea floating in the air and heading into her brain.

In a serious tone, Callie falls back into her role as unofficial group leader.

"Lucy, you will send the video to Mr. Horvik tonight, right?" Callie asks, as if I never thought of this idea before. She continues, "Our video is a-mazing and needs to get to Mr. Horvik tooo-night."

"Yep," I say with confidence. I lift my chin slightly and stand up straighter. Almost like a soldier addressing their commander. Except I have a huge smile on my face and my right hand is held high as if I'm taking an oath.

The group asked me to email our video. I always follow through, especially when I know people are counting on me. It's true. My group already put their faith in me by agreeing to combine groups.

Thinking back, it was so nice of Elizabeth to tell Mr. Horvik about the changes and why she dropped out of the project. I still feel a little bad about how it all went down. After all, Elizabeth is the one who loves to be in the spotlight. Her flare for acting would have helped. I guess I'll check with her tomorrow and ask when her next show is. Maybe Callie and I can go and watch her. You know, to show support.

Callie, Nolan, and I say our usual goodbyes and head up our own driveways. My mom is home already from work.

"Hi, Mom! I'm home!"

"Hey, Lucy! Forgot to tell you Levi has an early baseball game tonight. Dad has to work late. I'm running Levi to his game. I need you to empty the dishwasher and run this casserole over to Mrs. McCormick's house. Her mom passed away, so I wanted to drop off a meal for the family." Mrs. McCormick, Nolan's mom, is so nice. I want to help, but I have a ton to do.

"Mom, I have way too much homework. And I have to email our video project to Mr. Horvik ASAP! Why can't you drop it off on your way when you take Levi?"

"Lucy, I don't have time for this. It's only a few doors down. Now go without any more whining. I love you. Oh, and I made a casserole for us, too. It's on the stove. Help yourself and put away the leftovers after you eat."

My mom and Levi rush out the door with a water jug and sunflower seeds in hand.

Should I eat first or take the casserole over to Nolan's house? I guess if I take 'shine your light' to heart, I should head over first before I eat.

Walking to Nolan's house, my stomach growls more than usual. The smell of my mom's spaghetti pie is making my mouth water. I didn't have time for my full pre-dinner after school. *Although the lemonade and chocolate chip cookies from the coffee shop were delicious.*

When I arrive, Mrs. McCormick answers the door. She is one of the nicest people I know. She offers a huge smile and 'come in' when I get there.

We stand in the foyer, and I realize I'm never quite sure what to say after someone loses a loved one. If I bring it up, will I make things worse? Well, I guess I can't make it worse I mean, Nolan's grandma has already passed, right? *Ugh, I hate **uncomfortable moments** like this.*

Thankfully, Mrs. McCormick breaks the ice. "Lucy, your mom told me you were heading over. How thoughtful of your family to make dinner for us tonight."

"Ummm, I'm really sorry to hear about your mom." Mrs. McCormick smiles and I can tell she is holding back tears.

"Thank you, Lucy," she says and carefully takes the casserole dish from me. With her back turned, she calls out, "Nolan, Lucy is here! Look, her mom made your favorite dinner. Spaghetti pie!"

I don't hear Nolan say anything. Only quick footsteps are heard. He is even fast when flying down the stairs in his socks!

I hear a quiet, "Hi, Lucy," but he is not looking at me. His attention is only on the casserole dish in his mom's hands.

"Lucy, Nolan said he had a lot of fun at the coffee shop after school today. Thank you for including him in your group and always making him feel welcome. It means a lot to him. And to me."

Mrs. McCormick has me follow her into the kitchen. She carefully sets the warm casserole down on the stove, grabs a plate, and serves Nolan a huge scoop of spaghetti pie.

"Nolan did great!" I add. "He used one of his special voices. You know, the one that sounds like he should be voicing a movie trailer."

Nolan looks up at both of us and gives us a big smile, spaghetti sauce dotting the corners of his mouth and down the center of his chin.

"I need to head home for dinner and to finish my homework. Nolan, I'll see you at school tomorrow. And Mrs. McCormick, I'm really sorry…about everything."

She smiles, gives me a hug, and walks me to the door.

*I guess that wasn't as bad as I thought it would be. You know, having to bring up the death of her mom and all.*

Back at home, my stomach has gone from growling to full out roaring at the thought of the spaghetti pie waiting for me. Two heaping scoops and a big glass of milk later, there is no more growling or roaring. Only silence. The satisfaction of a delicious meal. I look down at my white shirt to assess the damage. *Not too bad.* Only three small spaghetti sauce stains dot my shirt. At least, they are spread out. *That makes it harder to notice, right?* I guess it's off to the laundry room for some stain remover. I think I need to invent shirts that repel spaghetti sauce for dinners like this.

I do as my mom asked (aka – put the leftover food away and empty the dishwasher) and start my homework.

I make my way to my room, lugging all of my school stuff like a pack mule. When I say I have 'work,' that may be a stretch. I have to unpack my school bag with everything from my locker. To be honest, I love locker clean out day. My locker is like a time capsule of my year. Pictures of friends; funny notes with inside jokes; a crinkled-up locker sign from my birthday in March; and a good luck sign from our volleyball conference tournament. Lots of reeds for my clarinet that I thought were long gone are also a welcome treasure buried at the bottom under some books, the ones I forgot to return to my literacy teacher, Mrs. Jacobs. A few empty candy wrappers, likely left from Halloween. And my favorite pen of the Golden Gate Bridge from my trip to San Francisco last summer. I knew it didn't go far! And the lucky rock that Callie gave me back in the fall when I was nervous about a math test. Not sure how much luck it brought, but it was a silly and thoughtful gesture from Callie. Each artifact from my locker brings such strong memories.

"Lucy, we're back!" Mom calls from the kitchen.

*Whoa! What time is it? My mom and dad tease me for being the greatest at daydreaming and putzing. They said if it was an Olympic sport, I'd win the gold!*

"What time is it? You are home so early!" I ask as I make my way to the kitchen for a snack (*I'm starving!)* and to say hi to everyone.

"Early? It's after 9:15 PM. What have you been up to? Hope you are done with your work. It's getting late. Time for you to shower and get ready for bed. Your 8th grade promotion ceremony and dance are coming up soon. You need to be rested for your big night."

"Ah! The ceremony. The video! Thank you! I **lost track of time** and almost forgot!"

I sprint back to my room. I'm about to grab my Chromebook when Levi walks in with a big grin on his face.

"Hey Lucy. Got a present for you."

"I don't even have time to get excited about this because the next thing I know, Levi is shoving his smelly, freshly worn, baseball socks in my face."

"GET OUT OF HERE YOU DORK!" and I lunge to push him out the door. My foot trips on something, but I catch myself in time. Both hands manage to grab on to his baseball shirt, stretching it from behind. Dad appears this time with that 'you two better knock this off right now' look.

I quickly release the back of Levi's shirt, sending him flying forward down the hall. *Ugh, I don't have time for this right now!*

I head back to my desk, and get the 'be the better person' look from Dad as he stands in the doorway. He leaves. Guess he's going to deal with Levi next.

The stench of Levi's socks lingers in my room. Seriously! What is up with that boys 'feet! Thankfully, I have a full line of body perfumes on my dresser. Nothing a few sprays of my favorite scent can't fix.

Finally, at my desk, enjoying the scent of Summer Dreams in my room, I start the email to Mr. Horvik. I let him know our double group video is ready. I also thank him for his understanding about Elizabeth leaving, combining groups, and combining topics. I attach the video next. It's taking a while to load. I hit send with a sigh of relief and close my Chromebook. I grab my pajamas and head out to take a shower. I'm so glad I can check that off my list. My friends will be relieved too.

If only I had known, then, when I lunged at Levi, it was the charger that tripped me. It was the charger that got pulled from the outlet. An outlet connected to the light switch that was not turned on. It was my charger that was needed since my Chromebook was only at 5%. And my video file was too large to send quickly. It was the charger that controlled if my email would send. If Mr. Horvik would get our video.

## Social Thinking

Sometimes, we are in situations that are tough. Tough situations are not just a kid or teenager issue. Tough situations are part of being human, and they happen throughout life. Lucy had to talk with Mrs. McCormick who was dealing with the loss of a loved one. For many people, this is an **uncomfortable moment**, not just teens. When talking with Mrs. McCormick, Lucy does the right thing. She said she was sorry to hear about the loss of her mom. Lucy used her social thinking to better understand how Mrs. McCormick was feeling. Lucy set aside her own feelings of discomfort to show kindness toward someone else who was sad and hurting.

## Time Management

This is a funny expression because we can't really manage time. Time just keeps moving. What we can manage is what we DO with our time. Lucy gets caught up with her own thoughts in her head and small distractions around her. This is called putzing, and it's especially easy to do when surrounded by your favorite things or technology like smartphones (with every app imaginable), tablets, and computers. These devices are not necessarily bad, but like Lucy, we need to remember that there is a time to work and a time to play. A time to help or do chores, and a time to relax and putz. A time to choose how you want to spend your time.

# Chapter 15
# Leave It on The Line

Second last day of school.

Our Chromebooks are collected during the first 30 minutes of school, and our lockers have already been cleaned out. We have a completely different schedule today with shortened classes. But these changes to our school day are OK. We are a day away from officially being high schoolers.

Sarah and I walk into the 1st hour literacy class. Mrs. Jacobs asks everyone to grab a few sheets of lined paper. Then, head up for the lesson.

*Seriously? A lesson!* It's the second last day of school. What more do we need to know? I wish we could just talk or play games.

"Students. Welcome to your last regularly scheduled literacy class of your middle school career. I know you have pushed your thinking and even surprised yourself from time to time as you **grew as readers and writers.** You have heard me say all year: Your words have value. Your words have power. You may not have Chromebooks anymore to type your ideas, but your words are equally powerful with a pencil and paper. Back in the olden days when I was in middle school – yes, the 1980s – my friends and I talked all the time. Without Snapchat. Without texting. Without any forms of social media."

A few audible gasps are heard throughout the room. Even from my partner, Sarah! Someone from behind me even says, loud enough for all to hear, "How did you survive middle school in the old days!" Laughs are heard throughout the class.

Mrs. Jacobs smiles at the drama from the students and continues, "Today, I want you to write yourself a note. Tell yourself why you value YOU."

Before she could go on, Mrs. Jacobs is interrupted by Elizabeth. "Are we just supposed to write a note on the paper you had us pick up?" Elizabeth looks across the room at Lola and rolls her eyes.

"I'm glad you asked, Elizabeth. As I mentioned, we did things differently in the '80s." From her pocket, Mrs. Jacobs pulled out what looked like a paper triangle. I think some of the guys make those to play table football. Slowly, Mrs. Jacobs unfolds the paper. As she does, the full note is revealed.

"These are my thoughts about all of you, my 1st hour 8th graders. I wrote about what I learned from all of you this year. How you asked questions that pushed my own teaching, and how I was inspired by so many of you who pushed yourselves every day to try new reading, writing, and thinking strategies, and how you made me a better teacher." She looks up at all of us and I think she may have tears in her eyes.

"In the center of your table are the directions on how to fold your note to yourself when you are finished. Please take a moment and think of one thing you have learned this year, or why you are a better person today than you were at the start of the year, or why you appreciate you."

After a few final directions, she finishes one last time with 'Off you go to write!'

*Here I go again. What to write? What to write?* Like always, everyone is back at their seat and has a pencil and pen moving across the paper. I can feel my heartbeat picking up. As I sit and think, my heartbeat reminds me that I improved my time for running the mile this year. And I am doing better in math because I'm asking questions. With these thoughts, my pencil starts. I don't even mind that some people are already finished writing and are working through the directions on how to fold their note.

Mrs. Jacobs walks around helping students fold notes here and there. She clearly was an expert note-folder back in the day. I finish my letter to myself and do a quick, basic fold and tuck my note into my pocket. I can figure out the fancy fold later.

## Social Thinking

When directions were given, Elizabeth jumped in when the teacher was talking. Elizabeth was interrupting her teacher. She forgot to use her social thinking, and wait for a time to ask questions. She could have raised her hand. Either way, Elizabeth was too busy thinking about what was in her own head instead of remembering she was not the only person in class.

Also, during school, when you work hard, something happens. You grow. Not just your height, but your skills. Most of your time is spent trying to learn new things, both in and out of school. Just like Lucy, it is important to stop and think about how you have improved your skills and what you are able to do now that you may not have been able to do in the past. When reflecting on your own skills, remember to celebrate what you can do! Also, try not to compare yourselves to others. This can be hard, but it is important to track your own growth and progress. Instead, look at where your skills started and measure how you have grown. This positive self-talk and thinking will help you set goals and be successful!

# Chapter 16
# The Lunch Line

The rest of the morning is slow. Time drags on. It's as if the clocks in the school are going backwards instead of forwards. Not much to do. Lots of end of year talk and announcements.

After what feels like an eternity, it is finally time for lunch. At least, hot lunch is my absolute favorite. Walking Tacos. I could eat them every day. I'd like to thank the genius who came up with the idea to take a bag of taco chips, add delicious hot taco meat, fresh salsa, gobs of cheese, and creamy sour cream, and call it a meal.

"It's Walking Taco Day!" Callie shouts from behind me as we walk. Well, it's really more like a slow run with a side of dancing mixed in, to get into the lunch line.

"Our last walking taco day of middle school. They better have these at the high school."

"Lucy, it is the same menu up there. Plus, you have softball season coming up, and every tournament will serve Walking Tacos, too. All. Summer. Long." We both do a little happy dance of excitement as we try to wait patiently.

The lunch line is already 30–40 students deep, and it's not moving fast. I look down the line behind me to see who else is coming. I see Nolan heading into the lunchroom with his favorite Spiderman lunch bag. Without even looking, I know what's inside: A ham sandwich on white bread with no crust, cut into triangles; tiny twist pretzels; a mandarin orange cup; and a fruit punch juice box. He has eaten the same lunch every day since he started at our school. Callie and I have tried to convert him to the deliciousness of walking tacos (and pizza, calzones, breakfast for lunch, and chicken nuggets for that matter), but he always replies, "No, thank you."

Nolan heads straight at us in the lunch line. Is he finally going to try hot lunch? "Hi, Nolan, want to join us in the lunch line?" I ask.

"No, thank you." Then with a smile, he hands me a folded piece of paper. It looks similar to the notes we wrote in literacy class this morning, but his folding is a little different. It's more like a basic square. Not the triangle origami fold Mrs. Jacobs showed us.

"Thanks, Nolan. Is this for me?" Nolan just nods, smiles, and heads to his usual seat in the lunchroom.

"What does it say?" Callie asks, as she is practically taking it out of my hand. I grab it back and put it in my pocket. We are getting closer to the serving station. I don't want any taco juice on my note. Finally, we reach the tray station. My stomach gives one last growl as I grab the bag of deliciousness from Mrs. Nell, our favorite lunch lady. I think she always gives me an extra big scoop of taco meat ever since Callie and I declared our love for this lunch menu item. Happy dance!

## Social Thinking

If you really like or appreciate something, say something. Lucy told Mrs. Nell, the lunch lady, how much she loves the walking tacos they make. Lucy has no idea what is in the note from Nolan, but his thoughtfulness made her smile. Often, it is the little gestures like these that matter. Recognizing others and reaching out to them makes them feel valued.

## Social Spy

Did you notice Nolan eats the same food every day? This is OK. For some people, eating the same thing every day is for medical reasons. For others, it is a safe, predictable routine. Regardless of the reason why, it is important to accept people for who they are and the choices they make (*as long as they are not harming themselves or others).

# Chapter 17
# Fall in Line

I don't even mind that lunch is over. My stomach is full and happy, and the entire 8th grade class gets to go to the gym to practice for the 8th grade promotion ceremony tomorrow night. My heart beats a little faster at this thought. *Me! Done with middle school. My first semi-formal dance! It's going to be epic!* This is one of those nights you wait all year for. During the school year, when the days are slow, the bus stops are snowy and cold, the tests are piled up…it's all OK because you have to get through some boring moments to get to the end of the line. This moment.

The gym is a combination of heavily scented body sprays mixed with the harsh aroma of teenage sweat, courtesy of the exceptionally warm spring and over-pumped teens basking in the knowledge that they are the top of the school. Teachers, trying their best to corral the 390 8th graders flooding into the gym, continue to repeat, "Rows are labeled alphabetically. Find your row and line up alphabetically by last name. Check the sheets at the end of each row if you need help."

The teachers already went through these directions before lunch, but I swear the information walked right out of our heads as the thought of walking tacos went in.

Mrs. Christopher, our principal, finds the microphone. She directs us to take a seat and finally manages to get the crowd to quiet down. Well, at least we quiet down after a few extra cheers and chants from the crowd. Mrs. Christopher walks us through our promotion ceremony so we know what to expect. We practice walking up to the podium while staying in our rows, and we shake hands with the administrators up front.

Next, Mr. Horvik tells us when the video presentation will be shared. As he starts the first few seconds of the videos to test the audio and sound quality, the crowd erupts into cheers as it blasts Logan and Asa's voices one hundred times louder than expected. Abruptly, the video stops. Groans of objection travel through the crowd.

"I'm saving this special tribute for the promotion ceremony. I'm very grateful to those who shared their time and talents to help create this. Congrats to all of you!"

My 8th grade class erupts into more cheering and clapping. Callie, Michael, Hayden, Jefferson, Anne, me, and the rest of my group look around to find each other in the sea of teenagers. When we do, we share a head bob and a smirk that telepathically says, "We rock!"

My heart races a bit more at the thought of watching our video in front of the entire 8th grade class plus everyone's family and friends. Like I said earlier: Epic!

The day ends with a final walk down to our homerooms. Student desks and chairs are scattered around the room. The walls are now bare, and teachers' boxes line the tables and perimeters of the classrooms. Students sit where they can find a seat next to their friends. No more seating charts on this last day of regular classes.

Mrs. Jacobs, my writing teacher, tries her best to keep students quiet as she hands out yearbooks. My 8th grade peers work attentively in their make-shift seats to perfect their best signatures followed by not-so-original catch phrases like **TTFN, HAGS**, Love ya! You're the best!

I absolutely love looking through my yearbook. The smell of the brand-new book. The sound of the new binding breaking ever so slightly as I open it for the first time. The fun memories flooding my mind as I look for my picture. But for now, that will have to wait. Time for signatures.

Nolan sits quietly at a side table, paging through his book. "Hi Nolan! Can I sign your book?"

"No, thank you."

"Oh. Well, will you sign mine?"

Nolan carefully takes my book, opens to the inside of the back cover, and with perfect vertical precision, writes, NOLAN.

"Thanks, Nolan!" He smiles and goes back to paging through his book. Before I can turn around, Callie's book is in my face.

"Lucy! Sign my book! Sign my book! And you better write a lot!"

*Typical Callie.*

## Social Thinking

Lucy does not get mad when Nolan doesn't want her to sign his book. She understands that for him, signatures will likely mess it up. He likes his book just the way it is. Lucy respects Nolan's decision even though it is different from her own. Lucy loves getting signatures for her yearbook!

This is why social thinking is so important. Two people can have different ideas, yet respect each other's choices.

## Texting Language

**BFF** and **HAGS** are common expressions used by teenagers when signing yearbooks, texting, or using other social media. They mean 'best friends forever' and 'have a great summer.' Students are not required to use these when signing a yearbook. Some students choose to sign their name and/or write a message with a funny memory from the past school year.

# Chapter 18
# Between the Lines

Back at home after school, my routine is the same. I prepare my pre-dinner one last time as a middle schooler. Then, I sit down with my yearbook. I love reading the comments. I always find it funny how some kids you don't even know that well sign BFF and Love ya! At least I can say they are friendly. *So. Many. Fun. Memories!* My volleyball picture with the school mascot we snuck into the photo (a stuffed elephant we named Spike) still makes me laugh. And I love looking at how people change from the start of the school year until now. Hair gets longer or shorter, braces come on or off, and even that zit on picture day that you thought would ruin your life forever has disappeared into history.

Still lost in my thoughts, I feel something poke my side as I get up off the couch to put my dishes in the dishwasher. It is the note from Nolan. I dry my hands and carefully open it. He printed every letter perfectly; letters tall and vertical. Each letter was spaced with precision across the light blue lines. Each word was spaced out the exact same distance from the next. As I start to read, I soon realize this is the note Nolan wrote in writing class this morning. Instead of writing a note to himself, he wrote one for me.

*Dear Lucy,*

*Thank you for always being nice to me. You always say hi, you cheer me on when I run, and you walk home with me. Thank you for always being kind. Good luck in high school. I hope we can still walk together.*

*Your friend, NOLAN.*

Tears fill up in my eyes as I read it over and over again. He's always so quiet. He usually only shares a smile instead of saying hello or good-bye. But **between the lines** of his written words, there are his real thoughts. I had no idea how much a 'hi' could mean. I guess sometimes you have to really listen to more than just words to understand someone. You have to listen with your heart.

## Social Thinking

You may not really know how someone thinks and feels just from their words and actions. Lucy had no idea how much her daily interactions impacted Nolan. There is an expression by Maya Angelou that says, "I've learned that people will forget what you said, people will forget what you did, but people will never forget how you made them feel." Lucy and Nolan are a great example of this. Nolan feels safe and respected by Lucy. Her kindness is an invaluable part of his day. He expresses his appreciation by writing this note to her.

## Figurative Language

**Between the lines** is an expression that means you sometimes have to look past the words. To truly understand someone or their ideas, you have to listen to their words, watch their actions, look at the situation, and use social thinking to see things from someone else's viewpoint. When people truly seek to understand someone else, respect and trust soon follow.

# Chapter 19
# Flat Line

The 8th grade promotion ceremony. This night is finally here! I know…it's not really a graduation. After all, we still have four more years of school. But this is a big deal! We are done with our grades as numbers. No more 1st, 2nd, 3rd, etc. We will now have fancy words like freshman, sophomore, junior, and senior in high school and in college. And we get to dress up. Most days, the halls are filled with girls wearing leggings and oversized t-shirts or sweatshirts, and boys wearing joggers and t-shirts. Dress shopping for this night was totally fun, although my mom did make me try on too many dresses that made me look like I should be living on a prairie or visiting an old folk's home. *I am not a fan of floral prints.*

I hear Mom yelling from down the hall for the third time, "Lucy, are you ready? Come outside so we can take some pictures!" I'm as ready as I'm going to be.

One last look in the mirror:

Navy blue A-line dress with halter top. Check.

Distressed, high-heeled tan leather sandals. Check.

Beautiful gold bracelet, a gift from my grandparents for this special day. Check.

Nails painted a perfect nude to match my tan (from softball weekends). Check.

Hair curled, falling just below my shoulders with a small braid to the side in the front. And plenty of hairspray. Check and check.

One last touch of lip-gloss. Done.

"I'm coming, Mom!"

So glad I practiced walking in these shoes. These heels are a far cry from my usual volleyball shoes, Crocs, and softball cleats.

Turning the corner into the kitchen, I see my mom and dad waiting for me. My mom clasps her hands at her heart and gives me the 'my baby is growing up so fast' speech. I know I see tears in her eyes, but try not to get emotional. My dad lightens the mood with his 'You look good, champ' speech. He's been my brother's basketball coach for years. I think he likes to fall into this role when he starts to feel emotional.

"You look nice for a girl. Don't do anything gross like kiss a boy tonight," Levi says as he contorts his face into a look of disgust after the word kiss. I guess this is the best I can expect from my little brother. Mom gives Levi the 'you better behave look' and we head outside by the garden for pictures.

It feels like a full magazine photoshoot. Multiple pictures with each family member. My mom is taking pictures each time I am not ready. My heels are sinking slightly into the damp ground from the heavy rain last night. After what feels like hundreds of pictures later, my parents, Levi, and I pile into our minivan. Levi left all of his baseball stuff on MY seat in our minivan.

"Slide your smelly, dirty baseball equipment over so I can sit down!" I say with a bit too much attitude.

With an overly dramatic heavy sigh, he shoves his bag over, spilling sunflower seeds everywhere.

**"Levi! Mom, look what he did!"**

"Ugh, you two. Stop arguing!" Mom asks Dad in her 'nice but I'm actually really mad' voice to get the small vacuum while she grabs a damp cloth to wipe the sunflower seed salt off the seat.

With the mess cleaned up, we tried again. This time, my family and I make it not only out of the driveway, but all the way to school without any more drama.

"Dad, can you please drop me off at the front doors so I can meet up with my friends?" I ask as nicely as possible. *It was a rough start to get here.*

Dad obliges and drops me off at the main door so I can get out right away.

"Luuucyyyyy!" Callie yells while running down the hall towards me with her arms open wide. She gives me a quick hug, then spins me around.

"You. Look. Ma-va-lous! Even with that sunflower seed stuck to your butt."

"Ugh – Levi!"

But I am in too good a mood to be annoyed or bothered by a small sunflower seed stuck on my dress. One swipe of my backside sends the seed flying. I am good to go.

"You look so pretty, Callie! Your updo is stunning!"

It really is. She had her hair done at the new salon next to the coffee shop in town. Her curls are pinned up loosely with diamond studded hair pins (well, not real diamonds, but they were very sparkly) – beautiful.

We walk arm in arm and find the rest of our crew toward the entrance of the gym. Michael, Hayden, Jefferson, and Mario look handsome in their crisp white shirts and bow ties. I think Hayden catches my glance, my a-bit-too-long glance.

*Stop staring, Lucy.*

Blushing, I quickly turn my attention to another spot down the hallway. I see Nolan at the other end as he walks in with his mom and dad. Nolan looks like he does most days. Cotton polo shirt, khaki pants, and tennis shoes. I can tell his mom put a dab of gel in his hair. He looks a little more grown up tonight.

I decide to walk over to Nolan and appreciate the chance to leave my current situation, along with my feelings of embarrassment, behind.

"Hi, Nolan."

"Hi, Lucy," he whispers.

"You look very handsome tonight. Are you excited?"

Nolan smiles, then looks from his mom to his dad, and back at his mom again.

"Lucy, you look lovely."

"Thank you, Mrs. McCormick."

My parents see us as they enter the big lobby, and head over to join us. They start chatting with Nolan's parents about how fast time is going, and they can't believe we are high schoolers. Parents definitely feel proud on a night like this.

"And thank you, again, for sending that delicious spaghetti pie over for us. Nolan ate every last drop of sauce from the pan," shares Mrs. McCormick.

Nolan turns to my mom with a big smile on his face. After all, he loves my mom's spaghetti pie. As the adults continue to reminisce about how grown up we all look, Callie pulls me back a bit so she can join our conversation, too.

"Lucy, this night will be epic. I cannot wait to see our video."

"I know, right! AND we have the dance after everything!"

We do our little happy dance as we think about tonight.

Teachers start filling the hallway, directing students into the gym to find their seats. "Parents and guardians, please, head into the gym. Fill in the center of the bleachers first. We are expecting a full house tonight."

I make my way into the gym and hear someone talking about their upcoming performance at our local community theater. Elizabeth. I turn around to say hi. She is surrounded by her group of friends, each with a more beautiful dress than the next.

"Hi, Elizabeth! I love your dress."

"Thanks, Lucy. You look really nice, too," she answers back.

***Wow, another compliment from Elizabeth!*** She has really **turned a new leaf** and is starting to be really kind. Maybe we will even be friends in high school.

"See you later at the dance," I say and head to my seat in the gym.

Mrs. Christopher starts the ceremony on time. There is such excitement in the air. Everyone is smiling, laughing, and even tolerating the million pictures requested by every parent. Marin, our class president, gives the first speech. It is lighthearted and funny. She talks about the teen years. Her speech serves as a reminder to students and a warning (in fun) to parents.

The ceremony slows down a bit as they call everyone up to the podium one by one for their certificate. All I can think as I walk up to the stage is 'Don't trip. Don't trip.' And I don't. No one does. It's funny what we worry about in life. We tend to hyper focus on the little things, issues that may never even turn into a problem. And sometimes, we miss the big problems waiting around the corner that should have been more obvious.

Fi-nal-ly, Mrs. Christopher introduces Mr. Horvik and welcomes him to the stage. Mr. Horvik's enthusiasm clearly livens up the crowd as he begins to speak. He shares a few words about how proud of the 8th grade class he is, and how inspired he is by the work the students produced for the video presentation. My class erupts into cheers and shout outs of admiration for Mr. Horvik.

*Goosebumps! I have actual goosebumps! I can hardly stand it. I'm so excited to see our finished video on the big screen!*

"And with that, sit back and enjoy the video presentation from this year's 8th grade class. Because, let's face it, we all want to see it, and the students want to get to the dance." The crowd laughs at Mr. Horvik's bad, but true, teacher joke as he presses play.

The gym lights dim and upbeat music, like you would hear at the start of an NBA basketball game, fills the room. The first video group is from Logan, Asa, Simone, and Amee. They filmed their video at the zoo and compared the big lions and tigers to the 8th graders, and then switched to the new baby lions and tigers.

"This is us next year. Even though we will have a lot to learn, we can and we will grow into our adult selves by senior year."

Super cute video! The crowd reacts with ahhhs and laughs at the right spots.

The videos kept coming.

*Where is our group video? Can't wait! Bet it's next. Maybe they saved the best for last.*

Waiting.

Watching.

*There's Lola, Stephen, Liam, and Molly's group.*

Waiting.

*What the…???*

*What am I watching?*

*Is that Elizabeth? On the screen? With my group's topic?*

Heart beating fast.

And with that, the video is done. The crowd erupts into yet another joyous combination of cheering and clapping. Students are high-fiving their neighbors who helped with the project. No high fives are sent my way. I notice my heart is beating faster now. Like really fast. Like, my heart can't keep up and might explode. Heads are turning in the crowd of students. Confused stares are coming my way from Callie, Hayden, Michael, Jefferson, Benny, and Anne. I see

Nolan sitting there, looking straight ahead with a smile on his face. He doesn't seem to be bothered, or even notice, that our video is missing.

Once the ceremony is over, I see the crowd clapping and cheering. I only hear ringing in my ears.

Students are dismissed by row to meet up with their parents. My video group is already waiting for me in the hallway. Looks of confusion and anger are daggers aimed at me. Everyone is talking at once.

"What happened, Lucy?"

**"Where was our video, Lucy?"**

"Did you send it to Mr. Horvik, LUCY? You SAID you would send it?"

"Seriously Lucy! You said Elizabeth wasn't making a video anymore and SHE was up there prancing around up on the screen like her usual dramatic self!"

Heart beating.

Heart BEATING.

Heart racing, heart racing Racing, RACING!

I see my mom and dad heading toward me through the sea of parents. I try to yell their name, but no sound comes out. I look from Hayden to Callie, to Michael, to Jefferson, to Anne. They keep asking questions. All at once. One person talking over the other.

Heart pounding in my chest. Can't find my words.

Breathing faster and faster.

I can't catch my breath.

*I feel dizzy. I just want my mom. Where is she?*

And then all is silent and black.

## Self-Regulation

Characters, like people, are complex. They can feel a variety of emotions within just a short period of time. Lucy is dressed up and on her way to her 8th grade promotion ceremony. She feels beautiful! Lucy quickly becomes angry with Levi for spilling his sunflower seeds on her seat as they head to the ceremony. Then, Lucy is happy again to see Callie and find her friends at school. Sometimes, when we are really excited, it is easy to become equally upset. Lucy needs to be aware of how she is feeling, both good and bad, and how she is managing a wide range of emotions.

By the end of the ceremony, Lucy needed help. She is confused by the omission of her group's video and feels a lot of pressure because it was her job to send the video. She ignored the signs her body was giving her. Lucy did not try to tell anyone how she was feeling, and then it was too late.

## Social Thinking

Lucy is aware Elizabeth is being extra nice before she enters the gym prior to the ceremony. Sometimes, when someone acts significantly different from how they typically act, they are up to something or covering up the truth. This is not always the case. Some people can change. But in this case, Elizabeth's behavior is very different for no reason. Lucy needs to use her social thinking and be aware of what Elizabeth says and does. Lucy needs to notice if anything feels off. Sometimes, people use the expression 'Trust your gut.' If something is off and not quite right, that usually means you are correct.

When there is confusion, or a stressful situation that impacts many people, there is a tendency for people to talk at once. And often, they talk at people. For example, Lucy's friends were all asking, **"Where was our video, Lucy?"**

When faced with this situation, and multiple people asking questions or talking at once, pause. Listen. Give yourself time to answer people. Try to find a solution. Yelling and accusing others does not solve anything. Instead, seek answers and solutions.

## Figurative Language

The expression, **turn a new leaf**, means to start over or act in a new way. Lucy is kind to think Elizabeth has changed; however, she should have used her social thinking and remember that even when Elizabeth has been nice, things don't turn out well for her (Lucy). It usually means Elizabeth was up to no good.

# Chapter 20
# End of The Line

22% left.

I've been on my phone so much today. Almost all the battery life I have is gone. And my life? Also at 22% right now. Or at least that's how it feels. How did I get to this moment? Everything was planned so perfectly. I made sure everything was done on time. I made sure my group knew where to meet…I followed the directions. I listened to my group members. But I missed one thing. One really big, super important, **flashing-in-my-face clue.** And now, while all my friends enjoy our 8th grade celebration dance, I'm stuck here.

In my bed.

All night.

Wishing I was there inside every photo liked on Instagram.

Looking at my dress, back in the bag, hanging on the closet door.

Shoes sticking out of the box. They still look brand new. But the blister on the back of my right heel is proof I wore them.

Mom's "Have some cocoa – you'll feel better cocoa" next to my bed.

Missing everything.

AND…

I think my little brother took my phone charger – AGAIN. The battery is draining with each swipe of post after post.

I wish I was there in the pictures on Instagram instead of here in my bed…

"Hey Sweet Pea! How are you doing?" Mom's gentle voice floats from the doorway.

"What happened? I want to be at the dance! And where is my charger? I swear, if Levi…" I say with tears filling up in my eyes.

"Lucy, you need to try and stay calm. You passed out. The school nurse said your blood pressure was off the charts! Does your heart ever race?"

"Well, yeah. All the time."

"Really? When? You have never said anything like this before."

"It's no big deal, Mom. It just happens, you know, when I get a bit stressed, I guess. Before a big test, when I get embarrassed, when I am called on and don't know the answer." *I guess this is way more than I realized.*

"Lucy, you need to pay attention to your body. And let Dad or me know when you start to feel stressed or overwhelmed. I called Dr. Martinez. She asked me to bring you into her office tomorrow. She said it's likely you had a psychogenic blackout. In everyday words, that means that you were so stressed and upset that your brain reacted by shutting down. This can also be caused by an anxiety attack."

"Anxiety attack! Great, just what I need right as I start high school."

"I know this isn't what you want right now, but that doesn't mean it has to ruin everything. There are a lot of things you can do to help yourself, and we can work as a family to support you. For starters, pay attention to how you are feeling and come talk to me when things get stressful."

"Fine. I will go see Dr. Martinez tomorrow, Mom. But right now I'm missing the d-d-dance." And with that, a flood of tears streams down my face.

"And I ruined everything, and my friends hate me. I don't know what happened to our video!"

"About that. I got a call from Mr. Horvik while you were resting. Your friends went to him and asked why he didn't include your group's video. He was confused because Elizabeth told him your group dropped out and agreed to let her do the whole thing."

"UGH! No wonder she was being so nice to me! She was living with the guilt of stabbing me in the back!"

"Lucy, you need to breathe and listen. Let me finish. Mr. Horvik checked his email, and pulled your Chromebook out of the LMC. There was no charge. Chances are your Chromebook died while you were sending the video."

"How could I be so stupid!"

"Lucy, you are not stupid. It was an accident. You are human like the rest of us. I'd like to say you will never feel this way again or be in another difficult situation, but that would be a lie. The truth is, life will give you plenty more ups and downs – great highs and painful lows. But we can help you manage and problem solve. We love you. You may be going into high school, but you will always be my Sweet Pea. Your dad and I are here for you."

My mom reaches over to hug me. "Mom!" I protest, but only for a second. I reach out and hug her back. And hold on tight for a long time. I feel safe for the first time in a long time. Mom doesn't pull away, but breaks the silence.

"While you drink your cocoa, I have something to show you that might cheer you up."

Mom reaches into her pocket and pulls out her cell phone, fully charged.

I can see the screen has an email from Mr. Horvik with a video attachment. I skim past the email part and go directly to the video and press play. I am expecting to see my video, but instead I see the crowd of my 8th grade peers, all dressed up and red faced from dancing. They seem to be facing the wall in the gym, but they are not looking at the mascot painted under the hoop. They are staring at the plain, empty space just to the right of the mural.

"Mom, what is this?" I ask.

"Just watch."

The video pans to Mr. Horvik standing in front of the crowd with a microphone. Surrounding him on both sides are all my friends from my video group: Callie, Nolan, Hayden, Michael, Benny, Jefferson, and Anne.

Mr. Horvik begins, "Ladies and gentleman. Due to some, ummm, miscommunication and technical difficulties, one video project was omitted from the presentation you watched just a little while ago. The value of this message is too important to skip. Besides the fact that this is a great video, the people in this presentation demonstrated what we want from every single person in this building, and, well, the world. Kindness, inclusion, teamwork, and determination. It is my pleasure to introduce to you the final video presentation."

Then, looking directly into the camera, Mr. Horvik adds, "Lucy, your crew thanks you for bringing people together and shining your light bright on all of them."

To my surprise, my friends don't look mad. In fact, it is the exact opposite. Callie is standing with her hands **forming a heart,** just like my mom does. The boys are giving me **a two-finger peace sign,** and Nolan stands with a big smile on his face.

I watch in silence, with tears down my cheeks. I am aware of the path each tear takes down my face. I am aware of the racing in my heart. I am aware of my mom's arms around me. I am aware of the warm spring breeze coming from my bedroom window that is cracked open. And I am aware I will need to let others know how I am feeling. But for now, watching this video, my heart is full.


## Self-Regulation

It took Lucy passing out in front of her peers to make her start to be aware of how she was feeling. Self-regulation is something we do every day. And by 'we,' it means everyone – kids, teens, and adults of all ages. We notice we are thirsty; we get a drink of water. We notice that we are hot; we push up our sleeves. When we are upset or stressed, we need to be aware of the signals from our bodies so we can use strategies to help us calm down and de-escalate. And this process doesn't end. As people age and find themselves in new situations, they need to continue to self-regulate and adapt to how they respond.

## Social Thinking

Adults have things to learn about social thinking just like kids. Sometimes, after an unexpected situation, it is easy to look back and wish you had done things differently. Mr. Horvik probably wishes he would have asked Lucy why her group dropped out instead of just listening to Elizabeth's story. He likely didn't do this because it was the end of the school year, and he may have been rushed to put the final video together for the 8th grade promotion ceremony. Lucy thought her friends would all hate her. In fact, it was the opposite of this. They were worried when she fainted. They felt proud to be part of her group idea that included everyone. Lucy also saw from her friends' body language that they were not mad. She saw Callie **forming a heart with her hands** and the guys holding up the **two-finger-peace sign**. Both of these gestures show care and support. Without saying any words, Lucy knew it would be alright. She observed the clues: Mr. Horvik's words, and how her friends handled the situation. We can start to see that Lucy's original thoughts (her friends hate her) were different from what was really happening. This is why social thinking is such a valuable life skill that helps us navigate social situations.

# Chapter 21
# Help Line

Whether you are 10 or 12 or 92, navigating social situations does not stop. We listen to spoken words, watch our body language and others, and monitor how others respond. This is big thinking work! But the good news is that you don't have to do it alone. Parents, guardians, family members, teachers, counselors, friends, and doctors are a great starting point. Seek help and ask questions if you feel stressed or anxious. Observe how others interact around you and surround yourself with people who respect you. When unsure of what to do next, stop and take a moment to observe your surroundings. Taking cues from others in social situations can be helpful. Here are some other tips and resources to help you with social thinking and self-regulation.

# Strategies to Help
# When Feeling Anxious

*Try a grounding activity like 5, 4, 3, 2, 1. Pause and name five things you can see, four things you can touch, three things you can hear, two things you can smell, and one thing you can taste.

*Get moving. Take a walk, stretch, lift weights or heavy objects. If you can't do big movements (ex: Need to stay seated), use a fidget, use your arms to lift yourself up off your seat, or wiggle your fingers and toes.

*Breath. Research shows that even three deep, slow breaths can reset your brain and calm your body.

*Get coloring. Draw, doodle, or use a coloring book.

*Listen to calming music. Try a variety of genres to see what works best for you: classical jazz, calming medication, sounds of nature, etc. Use headphones if you are surrounded by others.

*Talk to someone. There is no rule that you have to self-regulate by yourself. Seek help when you are unable to apply strategies on your own or your feelings continue to get worse.

# Glossary

**Figurative language**: Expressions that contain words that mean one thing when words are separated, but together, the expression means something completely different. For example, if you said, "She is a walking computer," that does not mean there is a computer with arms and legs moving around. It means the girl is really smart and has a lot of information.

**Self-regulation:** To be aware of how you are feeling and what you need. When tired, you know you need sleep. When you are thirsty, you get a drink of water. You do these things to keep your body and mind in balance. Your body gives you signs all the time: sweaty palms, a faster heartbeat, goosebumps, faster breathing, butterflies in your stomach, etc. Pay attention to the signs your body gives you.

**Social Thinking**: When you are with two or more people, you are in a social situation. You think about them and what they say, and they think about you and what you say. When we are considerate of others' thoughts and feelings, we are showing respect and kindness. This does not mean you always have to agree with people; however, it does mean there may be times when you have to respect differences in ideas and opinions. This is all part of social thinking.

www.ingramcontent.com/pod-product-compliance
Lightning Source LLC
Chambersburg PA
CBHW071349150726
47997CB00002B/916